Ashlynn

His Ladies with the Lamps
Book 5

By

Ronna M. Bacon

The Ladies with the Lamps

Matthew 25: 6-10

6 "And at midnight a cry was heard: 'Behold, the bridegroom is coming; go out to meet him!' 7 Then all those virgins arose and trimmed their lamps. 8 And the foolish said to the wise, 'Give us some of your oil, for our lamps are going out.' 9 But the wise answered, saying, 'No, lest there should not be enough for us and you; but go rather to those who sell, and buy for yourselves.' 10 And while they went to buy, the bridegroom came, and those who were ready went in with him to the wedding; and the door was shut.

Ashlynn

Deuteronomy 31:8

The Lord is the one who goes ahead of you; He will be with you. He will not fail you or forsake you. Do not fear or be dismayed.

Psalms 119105

Your word is a lamp to my feet and a light to my path.

NKJV

Table of Contents

Walking through her home that Saturday evening, Ashlynn Whitman was exhausted. She stood for a moment in the doorways of each bedroom, her thoughts on her four girls, as she called them. Two sets of sisters, cousins to each other, who she had been called upon to raise when the oldest was only twelve. She had willingly and gladly set aside her own dreams and plans to do that. Losing her beloved older brothers and their wives to an accident had been difficult but to learn just in the last months that their deaths had not been an accident but murder had almost devastated them all. Then, to have had the four girls face life and death situations had been so very difficult. She smiled slightly as she turned to walk towards her own bedroom, her soft peach dress rustling softly against her legs. Today had been Eilis and Declan's wedding. Her four girls were happy, finding their life mates, destined for them by God, during their adventures had been a surprise for all of them.

Ashlynn changed quickly, her good clothes put away, her shoes that she had been carrying in her hand on the shoe rack. She turned, tucking her T-shirt into her jeans. She hesitated, feeling a sense of danger and doom lurking in the corners. Shaking her head, she padded rapidly back towards the kitchen. She needed that cup of tea and soon, she decided.

Her hand on the kettle, she still hesitated, turning slightly before shaking her head. No, she decided, she had not heard anything. Her doors were locked up for the night. She fully intended to curl up on her couch with her cup of tea and vegetate as Darbi would have called it.

Only, she never got that far. Ashlynn turned back, filling the kettle and then setting it on the counter. She hesitated once more before plugging it in, thinking that she heard a noise. She turned to stare behind her, walking to the kitchen archway and staring around. Shrugging, Ashlynn returned to the counter, reaching for her favourite mug and then the tea caddy.

Only, Ashlynn never got that far. Another sound had her tensing and spinning. But she never made it all the way around. A hand was clapped tightly around her mouth, stilling the scream that had begun to build. An arm around her abdomen trapped her arms to her body. She was lifted up, struggling as best she could to escape, and simply carried from her home, through the back yard, and into the neighbour's yard behind her. That house was dark as they were away.

Set on her feet for a moment, Ashlynn continued to struggle. Her foot kicked at the man's shin but couldn't reach it. She tried to free her hands and couldn't. There was just nothing that she could do to escape, despite the desperate movements that she was making.

Ashlynn continued to fight to free herself. Her long dark brown hair with the red highlights had escaped from the clip that had gotten lost somewhere in her struggles. Her hazel eyes showed her fear but also anger. She just wanted to be free and wasn't.

The man picked up Ashlynn again and continued to pace forward, his face expressionless. He had not expected her to fight as she had. He had been assured that she would not and would be very docile. That in fact was not the case. He could feel the pain from the limited number of blows that she had been able to achieve.

A door opening in a nearby house caught his attention and he stomped that way, walking into the house, the door closed and locked behind him. He nodded as the woman simply pointed, continuing to carry Ashlynn.

Ashlynn was set on her feet in a room and the man stepped backwards. She spun around, anger on her face, her mouth opening and then closing without her words coming out. She stood, her eyes on the man, hearing movement around behind him but not seeing anyone.

The door was closed behind the man as he disappeared. Ashlynn stood for another moment before she was frantically searching for a way out. Her socked feet flew across the floor before she was tugging at the door, turning then to the window. She was on the first floor, she thought. *If I can get out of the window, then I can get away.* Only, the window was locked and couldn't be opened. She stared in disbelief at the lock on the window track. This doesn't happen.

The man walked through to the office in the house, rubbing at his shoulder. It had been hit many times by Ashlynn's head. He had not expected a woman of her age to fight like she had. She was to be docile and not fight back. That was what he had been told.

The woman sitting at the desk looked up, a frown on her face at being disturbed.

"She's here, ma'am." The man didn't look at his employer. None of her employees did. That was driven into them from the start of their employment.

"All went well? She was on her own?" The woman's attention went back to her paperwork.

"Not really, ma'am. She fought me."

"Did she? Well, of course she would. Now, go. Be back in the morning. She'll be moved at that point."

The man nodded and walked away, thinking that perhaps this was not the work for him. At the moment, he was undecided what to do before he walked away from the house and just kept walking. The other side of the country sounded good. He packed what he needed, walked away from his apartment, and disappeared into the night. The taillights from his car winked as he paused at a stop sign and then kept driving. With his disappearance, any information on where Ashlynn was disappeared with him.

The next morning, the woman was angry. The man had not appeared. That had delayed what needed to be done. She was beyond angry. Another one of her employees had had to be called in. That never happened with her.

Ashlynn didn't turn from the window that she was staring out of. There was no point, she had decided. Let them force her to go with them. She would fight them all the way. There were footsteps behind her before arms were once more wrapped tightly around her. A hand on her arm startled her before she felt the prick of a needle. She fought as best she could before the sedative took over her body and she slumped, held upright only the man's arms.

She was carried to a car, dumped into the back seat, and then driven from her home area. She didn't see the twists and turns that happened before the car slowed in front of another building, across the town from her own. It was a manufacturing plant that had been abandoned in the last year, a victim of a falling economy and the change in technology that had occurred.

Ashlynn was carried in towards a room or tower, whatever it was called, and then just dumped on the floor. A weapon appeared in the man's hand, pointing at the figure who had risen to his feet and watched in horror. The door slammed and locked behind the man and his footsteps echoed eerily in the dead of the building.

The man stood for a moment, rubbing at his face. He could feel the whiskers that had appeared over the last week of his captivity. His deep gray eyes were troubled and shadowed. His hand raised to his red gold curls, rubbing at them, before he was across the room, on his knees, reaching for Ashlynn. She lay in a crumpled heap where she had been dropped, not moving at all. He turned her over, a surprised sound coming from his lips. He knew of her, had seen her around town and at church. Who had done this deed?

Torin Callahan reached to brush the hair from Ashlynn's face, his touch gentle. He looked around, knowing that he needed to get out of there and get Ashlynn to help. Only there was no way to do just that. He had tried many times over the last few days. The room was solid. The only way out was the door and then a window too high for him to reach on his own.

He scooped Ashlynn into his arms and then moved to sit on the pallet of blankets he had been allowed. He held her, not knowing what was wrong, but knowing that he just could not let her lie on the cold floor.

His eyes raise to the ceiling. *God? This would be a really good time for You to help me. I need to get this lady to safety. Only I don't know how I can. Only You can do that. Help me to help her, Lord. Her girls need her. And somehow, I think that our lives just became entwined together. Lord, protect us.*

Chapter 2

Torin paced the room, knowing each crack and bump in the floor under his sneakered feet. It was something that he had spent many hours doing, just pacing. He had no idea who had taken him or why. The only contact that he had with anyone, up to now, was twice a day when a bag of food and water was dropped inside the door.

He paused, his eyes on Ashlynn. She had not roused in the hours since she had been dumped on the floor. That worried him. He was desperate to get her away. Only that didn't seem like it would happen.

Torin raised his dark blue eyes to the window, seeing the darkness lightening, his hand running through his black hair. It was coming to morning. How many days it had been, he was not sure. His watch was sitting on his desk in his office. He had taken it off on the day that he had been taken, without a chance to grab it. His phone was set beside it. He frowned, trying to figure out just who it was and unable to do that.

That day, Torin had grabbed his bottle of water and headed for his backyard. He had turned to study the rambling two-story house that he called him. It was lonely at times. When he had purchased it, it had been with having a family to share it with him in mind. So far, that had not happened. He was saddened at times because of it but knew that he had to wait on the Lord for that to happen. He turned to pace through the yard, studying the garden beds and bushes. There was updating to do, he knew, but he just wasn't in the mood at the moment to do that.

Torin walked back to the back porch, a large porch holding white wicker furniture. It was a favourite spot of his, somewhere he could just sit and relax. At times, he even would work out there. Torin didn't flaunt his wealth. He was a multi-millionaire, using his wealth to better the lives of others instead of his own. He lived conservatively, without it being obvious that he was rich.

Hearing a slight sound, Torin turned, his hands raising into the air as he saw the weapon pointed at him. The water bottle in his left hand dropped to the ground as the gun pointed at it. He sighed to himself. What had he gotten mixed up in? This was not what he did. Not at all.

Torin hesitated for a moment, feeling another weapon jammed into his back. He moved forward and around the house, his eyes searching for a way to escape. Only there wasn't a one. He had no chance to run and doubted that he would have had a chance to outrun a bullet. And Torin had no doubt that he would be shot if he tried anything.

He watched as the vehicle moved through his town, heading for an industrial area. He frowned as he saw the plant that they were approaching. He knew the building, had in fact looked at buying it just recently.

Forced from the vehicle, Torin was forced to walk into the building and towards the back of it. He was stopped in front of a door and then shoved through, the door slammed shut and locked behind him. He stared at it, realizing that what had just happened to him had happened to many others. His prayer was that he would be on his own, no one else involved. But somehow, he doubted that would happen.

He began to pray, asking for peace in the situation and then for an avenue to escape. Torin paced through the room, finding a small ensuite that had been added. His hand rested on the stone wall of the tower, for a tower it was. He stared up at the window, just high enough so that he could not reach it. Torin knew that he was in trouble, deep trouble, without knowing why. And who knew when he would find out.

Dropping to the rough pile of blankets provided for him, his head rested against the wall. He stared at the door, willing it to open. He would need all the patience that he was known for, he knew, to determine who and why. There were many persons who could be involved.

Days passed, how many, Torin was not sure. He spent his days in prayer and thinking through the verses that he had memorized over the years. An enforced study, he decided. Only, he told the Lord that he could have done this better if he had been free. Thinking through this, Torin sighed and prayed for forgiveness. If the Apostle Paul could learn while imprisoned, so could he.

He saw no one other than the first man twice a day as food and water was dropped on the floor inside the door. On the odd occasion, a tray of coffee was provided, but that was rare. Torin would simply watch from wherever he was in the room, not saying anything, just observing. That had been his way of life. Torin watched and observed, learning from life as he put it. His parents had supported him in that. He had regrets that his sister was not there. She had developed cancer when a teenager and had not survived. That had almost destroyed him, to lose her. God had gotten him through that and Torin knew that God would get him through this.

Torin had turned that last day, a frown on his face. It was not time for a meal to be brought to him. He frowned harder as he watched a lady dropped to the floor, a lady who was not moving. His eyes raised to the man who was backing towards the door, his weapon now trained on Torin.

Waiting for the door to shut, Torin's eyes were on the lady. He was across the room, on his knees, assessing her. He frowned. He knew her, Ashlynn, although they had never formally met. He carefully gathered her into his arms and rose, heading for the pallet and moving aside some blankets so that he could carefully place her there. A blanket was tucked around her.

Torin was waiting through the day for Ashlynn to rouse. Only she didn't. He had gently felt her head and could find no area where she seemed to be sore. That left only one option, that she had been drugged.

Ashlynn began to move in the late afternoon, her eyes opening and closing. Torin was on his knees beside her, his hand reaching to stop her tossing.

"Ashlynn? Are you awake?" He kept his voice low, not sure if the room was bugged or not. He fully expected that it was.

"Where am I?" Ashlynn struggled to sit up, leaning back against Torin's arm. "This doesn't look like my home."

"It's not. You were brought here this morning. Are you okay?" Torin grew afraid as her face continued to pale.

"I'm going to be sick."

Torin was on his feet, Ashlynn in his arms. He strode to the washroom, set her down on her feet, and closed the door behind her. He moved to stand against the opposite curved wall, his eyes on the ceiling. He was afraid, he admitted to himself and God, that she was hurt and needed medical attention, medical attention that she would not receive.

Chapter 3

Ashlynn cupped her hands under the running water and used that to try and rinse away the acid taste in her mouth. She had no idea what she had eaten or drank that had caused her to be sick. Whatever it was, she fully intended to avoid it in the future. She rinsed off her face, drying her face with some paper towels. She turned to the door, her hand shaking as she did so. She was not steady on her feet and that scared her. Ashlynn had no idea where she was or why.

Opening the door, she stumbled as she walked across the floor to drop back down on the pallet. Ashlynn simply laid down again and pulled a blanket over her. She heard soft rustling and then felt an arm around her, holding her upright and helping her to drink from a bottle. She was asleep again before she could mutter more than a soft thank you.

Torin held her for a moment, her head resting against his shoulder before he shifted her to the pallet again. The blanket tucked around her, his hand rested against her hair, a prayer rising for her. He was on his feet, pacing, anger rising in him for a moment at how she was in the situation that she was in.

The door opened slightly and the nightly meal was dropped on the floor as well as a cardboard tray holding two take out cups. Torin watched closely, seeing that the man wasn't looking at him. His eyes were on Ashlynn instead.

Torin finally grabbed a blanket and wrapped it around himself, seating himself on the floor, back to the wall, near to where Ashlynn slept. He wanted to escape, more than he had before, but that he didn't see happening. He finally slept, his head back on the wall. He didn't hear Ashlynn rising in the middle of the night, wandering the room and trying the door.

Ashlynn stood for a moment, staring down at Torin. She recognized him as someone from her church but not one that she knew at all. She didn't know if they had ever been introduced. If they had been, it must have been years ago. She curled up on her side on the pallet once more, the blanket pulled tight around her. She had no idea who had taken her or why. That was a fact she was desperate to find out. Maybe Torin would have an idea. The effects of the drug caused her eyes to close and she slept once more.

Torin was on his feet early in the morning, searching once more for a way out. He heard the door open and close and the food bag dropping on the floor. He didn't turn. There was no point, he decided. His eyes were on the window in a contemplative manner and then on Ashlynn. Maybe, he thought, he could lift her up to the window and she could break it and escape. He sighed to himself. That not likely would work. He turned as he heard a throat clear behind him.

Ashlynn had been awakened by the closing of the door. She had searched the room from her barely opened eyes. Torin had caught her attention and she watched him before she was on her feet.

"Excuse me. Is there a way out of here?" Ashlynn's winced at the abruptness of her words. She opened her mouth to apologize, snapping it shut as Torin grinned at her.

"Good morning, Ashlynn. No, I am not aware of any way out, other than the door and that window." He pointed at the window.

"That's rather high, isn't it?" Ashlynn's head tipped back to look at it. "Who did this?"

"I have no idea. Do you?" Torin gave a quick grin as Ashlynn stared at him. "I guess that's a no."

"It is." She stared up at him, a frown on her face at his height. She was tall for a lady but he still stood taller than she did. "How long?"

"For you?" At her nod, he paced away and then back to stand in front of her. "Less than a day for you. You appeared late yesterday afternoon. It looks as if you were drugged. This is the first that you've really been lucid."

"It is? I don't remember that. What about you?" Ashlynn paced the room, her hand running along the rough stones.

"Me? I'm not sure. What day is it?" Torin had lost track of time.

"Today? It's Sunday." Ashlynn stopped, wrapping her arms around herself. Her face grew sad. "Yesterday was Eilis' and Declan's wedding. I disappeared from my home in the early evening."

"I see. Then I've been here for about a week then, I gather. I have no idea why."

Ashlynn nodded before heading for the bag at the door. She opened it to find the food and then reached for the tray of coffee.

"They do this?" She turned to find Torin behind her.

"They do. Twice a day. I don't always get coffee or tea. Usually they just give bottles of water."

"I see." Ashlynn paced, her thoughts on her family. "I need to find my girls. I mean, other than Eilis. She's away on her honeymoon. But the other three will be worried. We were to get together today for lunch."

"Guess that's not happening." Torin simply took the bag of food from her, dropping it on the pallet, and swept her into a hug. "I'm sorry, Ashlynn."

Ashlynn was shocked for a moment at his hug before she hugged him back. She felt as if she had come home, to someone who had been waiting for her and for whom she had been waiting. *God, is this You? Are You doing this?*

Ashlynn moved away from Torin, her emotions in a muddle, she thought. She knelt by the pallet, sorting out their food. This was not what she had expected, not at all.

Torin watched her closely, not sure how she was reacting. He didn't know her and didn't know how to read her. He knew that he had that issue with the ladies. He just wasn't comfortable around them, except for Ashlynn. That puzzled him greatly.

Ashlynn twisted the cap back onto the water bottle, staring down at it. She didn't know what to say, how to start the conversation that was needed. Torin watched her before he began to pray, his hand reaching for hers. Ashlynn jumped at his touch and then relaxed.

"Torin?" Ashlynn stared up at the window, seeing the darkness coming in. She had slept on and off all day. "How do we get out of here? Can we reach that window at all?"

"Not likely. Even if you were to stand on my shoulders, we don't have anything to break it with. It's a solid window and doesn't open."

"Scratch that idea, then." Ashlynn drew in a deep breath, almost a prayer, she thought. "Why?"

"Why? I'm not sure that I can answer that, Ashlynn. I'm not sure that you could either. I have no idea who nabbed me from my backyard. I didn't recognize him. And from what you said, you didn't get much of a chance to look at the men."

"No, I didn't. It was just so strange. I was taken to a house in my neighbourhood. A couple of streets over from where I live." She looked up at him. "Where's your home?" When he said the street, she paled. "That's the house, Torin. That's the house that they took me to."

Torin stared at her in disbelief before he nodded. Someone was plotting in a deep and devious manner against the two of them. He needed out of there to determine why. He did have documentation with his father and his lawyer, that if he disappeared for any length of time, an investigation was to be started. He knew that would already be done.

Ashlynn suddenly yawned, still feeling the effects of the drug. She reached for her blanket, wrapping herself in it, before she settled down on the pallet. Torin watched her, knowing that somehow she was entwining herself in his heart. Only, he didn't want to acknowledge that. He was sure that she was dating someone. She had to be, he thought.

Chapter 4

Three days passed like this. Ashlynn was growing weary of being locked up. She worried about her girls, as she called them. Watching Torin, she wondered at his calmness and peace. She needed that.

Torin watched Ashlynn in return. He could see that she was recovering from the drugging, if that was what had happened. And he had no doubt that it had. He paced the room, trying the door on multiple occasions and then standing staring at the window. Even if they could reach it, they had nothing to break it with.

Ashlynn turned late that afternoon from where she had been standing in the centre of the room. She was deeply puzzled at why she was there or even why Torin was. He couldn't tell her. They had spent the days in desultory conversation, not sure if they would be in contact once they were released.

Torin sighed, knowing that they had to get away. Only he had no idea how that would happen. He stood staring at the door as he heard the lock click and the door open. Two men stood there. This was highly unusual, he knew. It was not the time of day when a meal came. Even if it was, there was only one man who appeared, not two, unless of course one of the men stood out of sight.

"Walk this way." The first man's coarse voice sounded loud in the room.

Ashlynn moved closer to Torin, seeking protection from him. His hand reached for hers, grasping it tightly.

"Move!" The harshness of the word whipped at them even as a weapon was pointed at them.

Torin approached them, keeping between them and Ashlynn, desperate to protect her. They followed the first man through the building and towards a vehicle that was waiting. Forced inside, Ashlynn shifted as close to Torin as she could, fear on her face. She had no idea what was planned but she didn't think that it was for their good.

Torin watched out of the window, wishing that he could escape with Ashlynn. His wishes turned to prayers, knowing that God was in control and would free them when He was ready. He felt Ashlynn tight to him and tightened his grip on her hand. He had no idea where they were heading, but he could feel the fear rising in him.

Ashlynn paled as she saw the direction that they were heading. It was towards the edge of town and towards a conservation area. This is not looking good, she decided. Her hand tightened on Torin, and she stared down at it. She didn't do this, she knew. She never dated, had had no desire to do that, not while she was raising her nieces. She certainly did not hold a man's hand. Yet, here she was, doing just that.

Forced from the vehicle and made to walk towards the woods, Ashlynn bit her lips to keep from crying out. The ground was rough under her sock feet. She had no shoes and she didn't think that she would have been given any. Torin stared at her and then down at her feet, anger rising in him once more. This was brutal, he decided. There was no need for this.

"In there." The first man pointed towards a shack. When neither one moved, there were brutal shoves from the man behind him. "In there. And no talking."

Forced to the dirt floor, their hands were bound behind them. Torin watched as the men walked out of the door, the door shoved shut and a stick bracing it closed. They could hear the footsteps fading.

"Torin? What just happened?" Ashlynn blinked rapidly to drive down the tears that she could feel tickling at her eyes.

"We were left here." He struggled with his bonds, not able to loosen them. He searched the room, managing to struggle to his feet. He could not find anything to help. Torin turned as he felt something bang into him.

Ashlynn stood beside him, nudging his arm.

"Here, turn back to back. Maybe one of us can loosen the rope. We can only try."

Torin felt Ashlynn's fingers as she worried at the rope. He could feel it giving bit by bit before he was able to free one hand. He reached to hug her before he turned her around and worked on her bonds.

When both were free, they stared at each other. Did they really just do that? Ashlynn headed for the door, shoving against it.

—

"It's blocked, Torin. How do we get out now?" Ashlynn turned in despair to him.

"Let me try." He shoved at the door, feeling it giving bit by bit. Finally, there was space enough for Ashlynn to slip out.

She stared around, not seeing anyone before she shoved the door back and pulled away the stick bracing it. Torin was out and beside her, a hand reaching for hers and pulling her away from the shack. They ran for shelter, stopping to stare back at the shack and then at one another.

"Where are they?" Ashlynn ducked her head to stare under a branch. "Did they just leave us?"

"It would appear that they did." Torin glanced up at the sky. It was starting to cloud over. "Come on. Let's see how far we can get before the rain starts or it gets dark. I'm sorry that you don't have shoes."

"I wasn't wearing any when they took me. I never do at home." Ashlynn drew in a deep breath. "It's okay, Torin. Let's just keep moving."

The couple walked forward, Ashlynn beginning to limp without being able to do anything about it. Torin watched her carefully before searching for a place for them to rest. He finally pointed towards a trail.

"In there, I think, Ashlynn. If I can remember correctly, there should be a cabin in there. It belongs to a friend." His forehead wrinkled for a moment. "At least, I think it's a friend."

Torin stopped their steps, his eyes on the cabin, seeing nothing that alarmed him. He tugged her forward, stopping at one point to reach for a hidden key. Unlocking the door, he waited for her to enter before he turned and walked around the cabin, returning to enter and then shut and lock the door.

Ashlynn stood in the centre of the cabin, searching it. It was rough, she had to acknowledge, but homey. She turned towards the kitchen area, opening cupboards until she found tea and coffee.

"Ashlynn?" Torin stood near her. "It's okay. The water is from a well but it's treated. Sam would say to go ahead with this. I think he has a phone here somewhere that we can use. There is electricity. He set up solar panels to do that."

"I see." Ashlynn opened the fridge, finding food. "He has food here. He must be coming back."

"He usually comes out here on the weekends. He needs that getaway."

"Who is he?" Ashlynn paused and turned to study Torin when he didn't speak. "Torin?"

Torin shook his head, returning to the present. He had watched Ashlynn as she worked away to prepare a meal for them, seeing her doing that in his own home for the rest of their lives. That would not happen, he decided. She had to have a boyfriend somewhere, he thought.

"Sorry, Ashlynn. What did you ask?" Torin took the plate with his food with a quiet thank you.

—

"Who is he?" Ashlynn pulled back a chair and sat, a sigh coming from her as she took her weight off her feet. They were beginning to be very painful.

"Who is he? He's Sam Blackier. A friend from another town."

"I see. Do I know him?" Ashlynn bit into her sandwich, her eyes not leaving Torin.

Torin shook his head.

"I'm not sure. I know he's been to church with me, but I'm not sure that he was ever introduced. He lives in a nearby town which, by the way, we are close to. That's what they did when they moved us."

"They did? I knew that we had left our town. How do we get home then?" Ashlynn dropped her sandwich back on the plate, her appetite suddenly disappearing.

Chapter 5

Torin paced the cabin late that night. Ashlynn had finally curled up on the couch and slept. He had found a blanket and draped it over her, a hand resting on her hair for a moment as he prayed for her. He had no idea how they were to get home and that worried him. Torin wrapped himself in a blanket and then just found a chair to sit in. He had no intention of moving too far from the lady with him. He just couldn't do that.

He was puzzled, that much was obvious. He had no idea who had taken him and then Ashlynn. He had not recognized the men. Torin's thoughts finally turned to the verses that had been rolling through his mind over the last ten days. Then he began to pray, his eyes on Ashlynn. He needed to get her home and just had no way.

Torin had searched for the phone, not prying into cupboards but just where he knew it was usually kept. He could not find it. He had sighed to himself, before his eyes had turned to Ashlynn. She had been sitting on the couch, her face in her hands. He wasn't sure if she was praying or crying. He just couldn't ask her.

Finally falling asleep, Torin didn't hear the car pulling to a stop near the cabin. It was early morning, the sky just beginning to lighten from the rising sun. The man stood for a moment, a frown on his face as he saw faint light coming from the cabin. There shouldn't be anyone here, that much he knew.

Sam walked around the cabin, a frown on his face. There was no vehicle, which there should be if someone was here. He quietly unlocked the back door and steppe through, blinking for a moment in the soft lighting. He frowned again as he saw a man sitting in the chair before he walked towards him. His frown cleared away as he recognized Torin.

Torin, what did you do? Where is your vehicle? I heard that you were missing. Your brother and father reached out to me, asking if I had seen you. Sam turned back to the cupboard, reaching to make coffee before he turned and walked back to the living room area, sitting near Torin. That was when he noticed someone sleeping on the couch. His head tilted as he studied the lady before shaking his head. He didn't know her. What had Torin done?

Torin roused at a slight noise, blinking as he looked around. His gaze stopped on Ashlynn. *No,* he thought, *it wasn't her. She's still sleeping. What woke me up?* He continued to search with his eyes, stopping on Sam as he sat, his eyes closed.

"Sam? When did you get here?"

Sam looked up, his thoughts dark for a moment. Something had happened to Torin, he could tell that.

"You look rough, my friend."

"I feel that way. It has been a horrible ten days or so. When did you get here?" Torin was on his feet, heading for the kitchen and the coffee that he could smell.

"About thirty minutes or so. Where's your car?"

"At home. I have been kidnapped, kept away from everyone, and then dropped off at the Millar shack yesterday. Ashlynn there appeared four days ago. She has no idea why. She was drugged." Torin paused to sip from his mug. "Neither one of us knows why. We were just over here late yesterday."

"Ashlynn? Do I know her?" Sam twisted his head to study Ashlynn, seeing her starting to rouse.

"I don't think so." Torin stared at the floor. "We have no phone, Sam. We need to contact someone."

"I know you do. I had to take the phone from here last time. There were issues with it and I was planning on replacing it."

Torin nodded, on his feet to crouch beside Ashlynn, who had roused enough to realize that they were not alone.

"Torin? Who's here?" Ashlynn's voice held her fear, something that she struggled to hide.

"Sam's here. He's been here for a while. Did you have a good sleep?" Torin grinned at her snort, something that he had not expected from her.

"About like that." She stared down at his mug and then simply swiped it from him, sipping at it as she sat up.

Torin stared at her in shock even as Sam began to laugh. Neither one of the men had expected her to do that.

"That was my coffee." Torin choked back a laugh.

"I know. Thank you." Ashlynn squinted in the low light. "Can we turn on more lights? It's dark in here."

"We can." Sam was on his feet, doing that and then moving to prepare another mug of coffee for Torin.

"Thank you." Ashlynn was on the move, heading for the washroom and a cloth to wash her face. She felt grubby and grumpy. She sighed, knowing that she would have to apologize. She leaned against the door, struggling for a moment to control her emotions. She knew that her girls would be beside themselves with worry. She needed to call them and soon.

Torin watched her before Sam touched his arm.

"She's hurting, Torin. And not just from this."

"No, it's not. Her four nieces went through some pretty bad stuff in the last year or so. Not only that, she became guardian to the four girls when she was only about 22. There are two sets of sisters. From what she has told me, the oldest, Brinn, was only twelve when their parents died. They had thought all along that it was just an accident but it has come out that it was murder. A friend of ours, Frank, a detective, has been investigating that." Torin stopped speaking, staring at the closed bathroom door. "I think it has all come down to Ashlynn. She's the reason why this happened. And that will devastate her. She adored her brothers and they adored her."

"I see." Sam stepped backwards for a moment, his hand on his phone. He handed it to Torin. "Here. If you remember his number, call him. You're still in his jurisdiction. He can investigate. You need to do that before you say much more."

"I know." Torin's head dropped for a moment as he tried to control his emotions. He knew that this would only get worse for Ashlynn and he just didn't want her to go through it on her own. Only, he had no idea how to tell her that.

"Tell her that you're there for her, Torin. I know your heart. You will not walk away from her. That much I know. She's going to depend on you just because of what you two went through."

Torin nodded, watching as the door opened and Ashlynn appeared. She stopped, her eyes on him before she was moving towards him, to be wrapped in his arms. She shuddered with her emotions even as she heard him praying for them both.

Sam watched and then nodding walked away, heading for the outdoors. He stared up at the sky, praying for his friend and his lady, knowing that their lives were intertwined now. He would not walk away from his friend, not at all. Only he had no idea how to help him.

———

Chapter 6

On that Sunday, Darbi had entered her aunt's house and slipping off her shoes, called for her. Flynn had followed, a box in his hands.

"Where do you want this, love?"

"The office, I think, Flynn. Where is Aunt Ash?" Darbi searched for her, hearing Brinn and Chani entering along with Gareth and Ronan.

"Darbi? Where's Aunt Ash?" Brinn stared at the kitchen, before she turned for the door. "She should be here. Her car is."

"I know. I didn't hear from her this morning. And she wasn't at church." Chani searched the house. "She's not here."

"No, she's not." Ronan stopped her from moving towards the kitchen. "We need to call someone, sweetheart. And that means we need to leave." He shared a look with the other two men.

Frank pocketed his phone as he approached the house, nodding at the three couples. This was not how he planned on spending his Sunday, that was a given. To hear that Ashlynn had disappeared was not what any of them had expected.

"What do we have?" He stepped into the house, a house where he had been present many times with his wife as a friend.

"She's not here. There isn't much to show what happened. Just an upset cup in the kitchen. The

———

backdoor was unlocked. The girls said that they hadn't heard from her after she left the clean up from Eilis' wedding." The patrol officer shook his head. "It's bizarre, Frank. After what her nieces went through, you would have thought that she would be safe."

"It is. Listen, have the techs come through. You looked through the backyard?"

"I did. I didn't see anything but that's not unusual. We don't know which way that she would have been taken out through." The patrol officer walked away.

Frank searched the house himself and then stood to watch the crime scene techs worked away. They shook their heads. He sighed. This had just gotten stranger, he thought.

Brinn wrapped her hands around Gareth's, her eyes on Frank as he stepped from the house. She was afraid for her aunt. She had had a bad feeling in the night that something was wrong. Gareth had simply wrapped her in his arms and prayed for her aunt.

"Brinn? Where is she?" Darbi huddled close to her sister, Chani on Brinn's other side. The four ladies were close. None of them wanted to call Eilis, not that they would have been able to reach her. She had simply grinned and said that they were going no contact for a week. They could try and call them but she doubted that they could get through. Where Eilis and Declan were headed was off the grid, she said.

"I don't know. I know that she wasn't at church this morning, but I didn't think anything about it. She was really quiet when she left yesterday."

—

"She was." Chani rubbed at her arms, feeling Ronan's arms around her. She leaned back against him. "She put her life on hold for us and now she's on her own."

"She is, sweetheart." Ronan's chin rested on his wife's head. "She is. She has to rethink who she is now and what she does. It's like she's become an empty nester and she is still young."

"She is. I never knew if she had ever dated." Darbi leaned back against Flynn

"She hadn't." Brinn blinked to clear her eyes. "She told me once that we were more important than that. That if God wanted someone in her life, then they would appear in God's timing."

"She would say that, wouldn't she?" Chani stared at Frank as he came to a stop in front of them. "Frank?"

"She's not there and not likely has been since yesterday." Frank's heart broke for his young friends even as he prayed for them. "How was she when you last saw her?"

"She was quiet, not like herself." Brinn sighed. "This has all been so stressful for her. What we went through. What happened to Dad and Mom and Uncle Adam and Aunt Leah."

"It has been. I talked with her briefly after she got home." Frank couldn't and wouldn't say why. He had reached out to Ashlynn, just getting her feelings for where she was at. She had been honest with him, simply stating that she didn't know and that perhaps she needed to go away for a few days. Only he knew that she wouldn't have done that without telling one of her girls.

"I think it's everything." Gareth spoke for the first time. "She's been through so much. She's not been grieving as she wanted to for what happened to her brothers. That has been weighing on her. She didn't need to say anything. I could see that. Dad and I talked about that last week. He's starting an investigation into that." Garrett, Gareth's father, was an investigator.

"I thought that he had already." Flynn eyed Gareth.

"He had but now he's moving forward with it. Ashlynn asked him to. He's reaching out to others to help."

"Emma for one, I know." Darbi wiped at her eyes. "Where is she, Frank?"

"I don't know, Darbi. I wish that I did. I'd go find her and bring her home for you if I could." Frank walked away after a few moments. He turned to watch Ashlynn's girls as they were known as. His wife, Sue, was a good friend of Ashlynn, had been since their college days. He sighed. He would need to reach out now to her boss, to see if there was anything there that would give him a clue as to where she was.

Adam, a fellow detective from the force, spoke from beside him.

"Ashlynn?"

Frank nodded. He was frustrated to say the least.

———

"It is. She's gone missing, sometime after she came home from Eilis' wedding. There is not much evidence though. We can't tell how she disappeared."

"You can't?" Adam was puzzled as well.

"That's right. Her shoes are there. Her phone. Her keys. Her car. The only evidence is an upset cup in the kitchen. The tea caddy was out, so we're assuming that she was planning on making a cup of tea and then likely curling up in one of her chairs in her sun room. That's her comfort room."

"It certainly seems as if it is, from what I have seen." Adam rubbed at his neck. "Does if have anything to do with Torin Callahan?"

"Torin? Why would you ask that? He's out of town, isn't he?" Frank turned to watch Adam as the other man shook his head.

"No, he's not. He's missing. From what I understand after speaking with his father, Troye, he's been missing for about a week. They only just realized that."

"He has been? Then, we'll need to look through his house."

"That's what I told Tam. He's to meet me there in an hour." Adam paused, a thought crossing his mind. "You know, his house is only a couple of blocks from here."

"It is, isn't it?" Frank grabbed at Adam's arm, rushing for their cars. "Head that way. I'm right behind you."

The three couples watched as the two detectives sped away before they exchanged glances. This is not what was needed, they all agreed. The couples finally turned and walked away, heading for their cars and then to Brinn's home. They agreed without words that they needed to meet, to spend time in prayer and then also to start searching for their aunt.

Chapter 7

Frank walked through Torin's home. He couldn't see anything out of the ordinary there, he decided, but he didn't really know the other man. He had never been in his home.

"Adam? Is his father here?" Frank paused in a bedroom doorway, watching Adam as he searched the room.

"He is. He's out by his car. I think we'll need to have him walk through once the team's done their work."

"I agree. Let me go talk with him and see what he has to say."

Frank walked towards the older man, a man in his late fifties, he decided.

"Mr. Callahan?" Frank reached out his hand to be shaken. "We'll need you to walk through the house for us. When did you last talk to or see Torin?"

"I can do that. I was through there yesterday, looking for him and not seeing him. I hope that I didn't disturb anything."

"It can't be helped. You didn't know that he was missing, did you?" Frank watched him closely, seeing the concern and worry Troye was trying hard to hide.

"No, I didn't. I had spoken to him last weekend. He had indicated that he was planning a trip this week at some point. That is not unusual for him. He does travel to some degree. It is also not unusual for us to

---

go a few days without speaking. I also spoke with his brother, Tyrel. He hasn't seen or spoken with him either. And that is unusual. The two boys are close, very close, and usually speak or text every day. Tyrel has been out of town since Monday and just got back. He called me, worried about Torin. There is no sign of him?"

"I'm sorry, Mr. Callahan. There isn't. Now, once our team has gone through, we'll walk you through. Your wife is here?"

Troye shook his head.

"She's not. She had to be with her sister out of town today. I wish that she was here. She's taking this hard." Troye wiped at his eyes. "Where is he?"

"We'll find him, Mr. Callahan."

"Please, call me Troye. Come get me when you're ready for me to go through the house." Troye turned as he heard footsteps.

Tyrel stopped beside his father.

"Dad? What's going on? No sign of Torin?"

"No, there isn't. Frank here wants me to go through the house. You're better to do that. You're here almost every day."

"I can do that, Dad." Tyrel turned to face the house. "Adam's working it?"

"He is? I didn't know that." Troye sagged against his car, Tyrel's hand on his shoulder.

"He is. I'm glad. Adam's been a good friend to us over the years."

———

"He has been. I have seen Frank around church. We've sat in some of the same meetings and spoken briefly. I guess we'll get to know him now in a professional manner."

"We will. We'll find him, Dad. Don't worry about that."

"I know that we will." Troye watched his youngest son closely. Neither of his boys had married and that concerned him, but he knew that they were praying through that. When God had the ladies for them, He would connect them. That was a fact Troye had no doubt about.

Frank walked back towards the two men, Adam at his side.

"I'm friends with Torin and Tyrel, Frank. Just for the record."

"I thought that. I've seen you with them at church. As far as I am concerned, it doesn't make a difference. I'm friends with Ashlynn and I'm investigating that. Our captain knows that."

"He does. Now, let's get them through the house. I didn't see anything odd."

"No, not really. But it did look like a lady's footprints there. In socks. That seems odd. He's not dating, is he?"

"No, he isn't. And that was odd."

Troye hesitated as he stepped into the hallway. The house had a closed up feeling, unlike how it usually felt. He walked through the rooms, Tyrel following him, and then headed for the back door.

Stepping through the doorway and onto the back porch, Troye hesitated. He could feel the evil that had hit here.

"He disappeared from out here, Adam. I can feel the evil here." Troye walked down the steps and into the yard. He walked through the yard, Tyrel walking towards him from the other side.

"Dad? Do you see anything?"

"Not a thing, son. Whoever it was didn't leave much. But then it's rained this past week."

"It has, Troye." Adam and Frank stood beside them. "We can't find any evidence of where he disappeared from. Did you look for his phone, keys?"

"I did. They're on the desk in his office. And if he was out, they would be with him. His car is also in the garage."

Frank ad Adam shared a look. This sounded so much like the scene that they had just left. It sounded like Ashlynn.

"Do either of you know Ashlynn Whitman?" Frank asked the question, studying his notebook.

"Mom does, I think. From their ladies' group. I can't tell you how well they know each other. Why?" Tyrel shifted his gaze between the two men. "She's missing?"

"She is. We just found out." Frank finally walked away, tucking his notebook and pen away. Adam had stayed, just to ask further questions.

Troye walked back through the house after Adam had left. He really didn't want to be there but felt that he had to. He pulled out his phone as he felt it vibrating.

"Troye? Any word?" Heather was on the other end of the line.

"No, love. I'm sorry. I'm at his house now. The police have been through. Adam is one of the detectives. He has just left."

"Oh, no! I thought that! I had that feeling you are always teasing me about. Hope and I are on the way home. Do you want me to come there?"

"I think not, love. Head for home." Troye locked the door behind him, Tyrel waiting for him. "The thing of it is that he's not the only one missing. Ashlynn Whitman disappeared as well sometime over the last few hours."

"Ashlynn? What? How can that be? After all her girls went through? We need to pray, Troye. I just had that really bad feeling."

"Me too. Listen, don't hurry but get here as quickly as you can. We'll meet. Tyrel said he knew one of the boys married to one of Ashlynn's girls. He's reached out to Flynn."

"He has? Good. Now, we're about thirty minutes out." Heather clicked off her phone, sharing a look with Hope.

"He's not there?" Hope's voice held worry.

"No, he's not. And Ashlynn is missing as well."

"Ashlynn? What is going on with that family?" Hope's attention was back on the road and the traffic around her.

45

Walking through the downtown area, Frank hesitated at the cafe before he was through the door. He stopped at the counter. The owner, Jeff, approached him.

"Frank?"

"Jeff, both Torin Callahan and Ashlynn Whitman have gone missing. Have you heard anything?"

"Not a thing. When?" Jeff handed over a mug of coffee, watching Frank closely as he sat on a stool at the counter. He leaned on it himself.

"Torin, we're not sure. Ashlynn? Within the last twenty-four hours. I was hoping that you had an idea."

"No, I don't. Not for Ashlynn. Now, Torin? With his money and his non-profit, it's possible that someone has taken him for ransom."

"That's what we're thinking. Let me know if you hear anything." Frank's phone was out and he was checking his messages and texts. Nothing, he decided, that helped. He was on his feet, heading for another crime scene, not that he really wanted to set aside Torin and Ashlynn. It was just that he had no option.

Jeff moved to stare out of the entry door. It was quiet for the moment in the cafe, with only a few customers. He turned and headed for his office. There had to be something that he could do. He reached for his phone, making a call and setting in process a plan

—

to help find the two and when they were found, to find the ones responsible.

Frank reached for his phone again, frustrated at how much it was ringing. He listened to the techs who had searched the homes. They had found nothing that would help. Frank sighed and then began to pray for his friend and for Torin. Somehow, their lives had become entwined. Just why that was, Frank wasn't certain of, but he would dig until he found out, as he knew that Adam would.

A few days had passed before Jeff's phone rang. He listened carefully and then was on his feet. He waved at his head waitress and pointed to the door. He had been told where the couple was and now needed to find either Frank or Adam.

Frank turned as he heard his name called. Jeff was running towards him. He frowned. Jeff never left his cafe at this time of the day.

"Jeff? You look like you are on a mission?"

"I am. I had word where they are. In the old carpet building. They're locked in the tower."

"The tower? Really? Okay. Head back for your cafe. I'll be by later to get your statement as to how you knew that."

Frank and Adam followed the ETF men as they moved through the building. They found the tower, the lock on the floor, and the room empty.

Frank stepped into the room, searching for anything that would show where Ashlynn and Torin were.

"Someone was here, Frank. I would say up until today. We must have just missed them."

"I would agree, Adam. Now we have to search further. Start with this building and its owners. They are likely buried in paperwork and numbered companies, if that is what I remember correctly."

"I'll head back and start that. We were just so close."

"We were. We'll canvas the area and see if we can find anything. But I'm not hopeful that we will. It's too isolated."

"It is, but there may be someone who saw something. It's whether they will say anything or not."

Frank nodded, his eyes on the pallet of blankets. *Is this all that they had, Lord? Just this pile of blankets?* He saw the one laying away from the others. *That would have been Torin, wouldn't it, Lord? Giving Ashlynn the most blankets. Help us to find them, dear Lord, and soon.*

Walking away from the building, Adam searched the area, following the tracks towards where a vehicle had been sitting. He frowned before shaking his head. There were four sets of footprints, including what he thought were a lady's. Only the lady's looked odd. He lifted his head, motioning one of the patrol officers over.

"Stu? These look odd."

Stu, a veteran officer who had been around the block many times as the saying goes, stared down at

---

the marks. He walked back towards the building and then back towards Adam.

"She doesn't have shoes on. She's in her sock feet."

"That's my reading. It has to be Ashlynn and Torin. That's what we were told. Any word on the street that you know of?"

"I haven't heard anything. And I should. The people are good that way. If it's Torin, he has done so much for the people. I know that they would be looking for him."

"That means they must be out of town somewhere." Adam rubbed at his neck once more, something he seemed to be doing a lot lately.

"I would expect that. Unless they have been moved to another house in town. And that is always possible."

Adam nodded, his phone out to take photos before beckoning over a tech.

"We need photos of these."

The tech nodded, having already been doing that as he walked towards Adam.

"We'll process what we have and then get the reports to both you and Frank."

Adam turned and studied the building, a frown on his face. *Where are they, Lord? Where can we find them? It's been too long already. I just want to know where to look. And I don't think that's in town, is it?*

—

The three young couples gathered that night at Brinn's home. They had shared a meal and then time in prayer. Gareth had been on his feet when they finished and returned to the living room with pads of paper and pens, handing them out.

"Okay, let's start working. I know that we have but we have to try harder." Chani blinked back tears. She was missing her aunt so much, she had told Ronan. She just needed her home.

"I know. Dad's weighed in." Gareth studied his wife, seeing the stress on her face.

"And?" Flynn looked up at that point, his pen tapping on the pad of paper.

"He doesn't think that they're still in town. He's looking outside of town for something or someone. He hasn't said yet if he's found anything."

Ronan nodded, having had the same feeling.

"Tag was around. He had heard what happened and is starting his own search. Evan talked to Emma and she's agreed that he can work it." Emma, a friend of theirs, had a company that found information on people that no one else seemed able to find.

"Emma has? Good. She'll work it as she can, knowing her." Darbi shifted on the couch. "We need to reach out to Eilis."

"I did. I left a voice mail for her last night. I don't know that she'll get it for a few days. She'll be so upset." Chani wiped at her face, her tears falling for a moment.

"She will be but we'll get through it."

The six young people worked away for a while before Gareth was on his feet, heading for the kitchen. He squinted at the clock. It was getting late, he saw, and knew that they would soon have to pack it in for the night. In the meanwhile, he would just prepare a snack for them. He turned as he felt a hand on his back and reached to wrap Brinn into his arms.

"Okay, love?" He felt her nod, knowing that she was fighting her emotions. "We'll find her."

"I am praying that we do. It's hard to trust in situations like this."

"It is. Listen, how be we meet with Dad tomorrow night? Just us?"

"We can do that. Your mom called and asked if they could bring a meal over."

"That's what they do. Now, have we made any progress?

Brinn shook her head, knowing that they had not really accomplished much.

"I don't think so. It's frustrating, sweetheart. I wish Aunt Ash was here. Do we know if there is anyone else missing?"

Ronan paused in the kitchen doorway, a frown on his face

"Why would you ask that?" Ronan reached for the tray with the sweets on them, watching his wife's cousin closely.

Brinn shrugged, not sure why she had asked that.

"I just wish that I knew for sure that she was okay. I just thought that if someone was with her, she wouldn't be so alone." She sighed again, feeling that was all she had done lately.

"I haven't heard of anyone." Ronan turned as he heard a sound from Flynn. "Flynn?"

"I just got an alert from our church's prayer chain. There is someone else missing. Torin Callahan."

"Torin?" Gareth blinked. He knew the man, having done work in his house. "I've worked for him. When did he go missing?"

"We're not sure. His dad put it out, I guess." Flynn looked up, staring at each one staring back at him. "Are they together?"

"They may be." Brinn was moving past them, reaching for an envelope that she had just set aside that day, not willing to open any mail. "I wonder."

"Wonder what, Brinn?" Darbi was beside her as Brinn set the envelope on the kitchen table.

"This. I just set it aside today. It's bulky." Brinn reached to open it, stopping as Gareth's hand rested on hers. "Gareth?"

———

"We pray first, love. Then we look at it." He was as good as his word, praying for what they would find and that Ashlynn would be home soon.

Brinn carefully opened the envelope, a large manila one, and dumped it out onto the table. They all frowned at the contents before Brinn set each item on its own.

"These belong to Mom and Dad and to Aunt Adam and Aunt Heidi." Eilis was disturbed.

"They do. To Uncle Aaron and Aunt Cait." Brinn was puzzled, staring down at the items. "There's Dad's watch. Mom's engagement ring. Uncle Aaron's class pin. Aunt Cait's birthstone ring. Who did this?"

"And what is this?" Flynn pointed to an object none of them had named.

Chani reached for it, using the tip of a finger to touch it.

"It's Aunt Ashlynn's. It's her bracelet that she got when she was 18. When did it go missing?" Chani stared at her cousins. "I don't remember her saying anything."

"She showed it to me last week." Darbi spoke up, tears welling in her eyes. "Whoever took her did this."

"Likely. We'll need to call Frank or Adam." Ronan walked away, his phone out. "Frank? Are you on call tonight or is Adam?"

"We both are. Is there a problem?" Frank squinted through the dimming light, trying to locate Adam.

—

"There is. We're at Brinn and Gareth's. Brinn received an envelope tonight. It has items from both sets of parents. But it also has an item of Ashlynn, one that Darbi saw just last week."

Frank's steps froze as he walked towards Adam, who was walking towards him.

"What did you just say?" Frank pointed towards his vehicle. The two men had ridden together.

"I said that there is a bracelet of Ashlynn that Darbi saw last week. They took it from her home."

"Okay. We're on our way." Frank dropped his phone into his pocket before he sat quietly for a moment.

"Frank?" Adam's voice finally broke through the quiet in the car.

Frank roused himself, shaking his head.

"Okay. So Brinn received an envelope with things of her parents and her uncle and aunt. However, there was also a bracelet of Ashlynn. One that Darbi saw last week."

"What? Did we search the complete house?"

"I think we did, but we would not have known if anything was missing. We need to go back through there tomorrow with the girls."

Frank parked in front of Brinn and Gareth's house and then just sat. His eyes were on the house, his thoughts a troubled mess he thought. *Where do we go, Lord? I pray for protection for all of these young people gathered here and for Eilis and Declan away.*

"I can do that. You're due in court." Adam reached for the door handle, not sure what to expect when they entered the house. This was just getting more and more bizarre.

Brinn watched as Frank stood at the table, his eyes on the jewelry. She could hear Adam speaking with Darbi. He was puzzled, that much she could see.

"Frank? What are your thoughts?" Brinn's question had Frank looking at her.

"My thoughts? That we need you ladies to go through Ashlynn's house, to see if there is anything else missing. I also need to reach out to the investigator in your hometown."

"I see. This is just so strange. I thought you had searched."

"We did, looking for evidence of what happened to your aunt. This changes it. We'll need to go back through the house again, just to determine if anything else is missing."

The next night, Frank walked through Ashlynn's house, not finding anything else missing as far as the girls could determine. That puzzled him. It was becoming more and more bizarre, he thought.

Brinn turned from locking the door behind him, not sure where they now stood. She walked into Gareth's arms. The meeting with his parents had been put off until the next night. There had been no question on doing that.

Finally walking away from the house, Brinn stared up at the clouded over sky. She was worried about her aunt but felt a sense of peace about her.

—

Two days later, Brinn stood in her aunt's home, hearing soft rustling sounds. She was scared but also determined to face whoever it was that was there. She walked quietly through the house, searching each room. She stopped abruptly at her aunt's bedroom doorway, not sure that she was really seeing Ashlynn.

Ashlynn froze for a moment, sensing someone else near her. She spun, a hand to her throat, before she was across the room, Brinn in her arms. She could feel Brinn sobbing.

"It's okay, Brinn. It's okay." Ashlynn's voice took on the tone that she had used when the girls were younger, a soothing quality to it.

"Aunt Ash? What is going on? Where were you?" Brinn shifted backwards to stare at her aunt, seeing the change in her face and not liking it at all.

"We'll talk, Brinn. Just not tonight. You're okay?" Ashlynn turned her towards the kitchen. "I could use a cup of tea and I know that you could."

"Where were you?" Brinn was not ready to let her questions go.

"Tomorrow, Brinn. Tomorrow. This involves someone else. I need to meet with all of you. Eilis was to be back in the morning. We'll get together for a meal and then talk. I have spoken with Frank and given my statement."

Brinn finally nodded, not happy with having to leave her questions.

"Do the others know?"

"I just had sent out a text message when you showed up. You should have received it."

Brinn sighed, having felt her phone vibrating in her pocket.

"I think I felt it come through. I was just so focused on what was happening here. Did Frank talk with you?"

Ashlynn hesitated for a moment, her eyes on the cupboard that she had just opened. Her hand rested on the counter as she heard the kettle beginning to whistle.

"He did, Brinn. He did. I don't understand it. And there doesn't seem to be anything else missing."

"It is strange, Aunt Ash. Are you okay?" Brinn took the cup of tea extended to her and then sat at the table.

"I will be, dear. Now, what have you been up to?" Ashlynn changed the subject, leaving Brinn to stare at her before she began to reply.

Ashlynn locked her house up after Brinn had left. She was exhausted, she acknowledged, but also acknowledged to herself that she was unlikely to sleep. And that was the fault of a tall, handsome man who had been around her the last few days. She had felt safe around him. Now they were separated. She wasn't just sure where they were going as friends. He had said that he didn't want to have her walk out of his life and she had said the same. He had dropped a kiss on her temple just before he walked away, heading for Sam's car.

Reaching for her phone, Ashlynn scrolled through her messages. She sent off a text message to her employer and got a swift response, simply stating that he was glad that she was safe. They would talk, he said, on Monday. He didn't expect her before then.

Frank had left voice mail for her, just stating that he and Sue were praying for her. Did she need anything? She smiled as she thought through the years of friendship they had all shared. She simply sent back a message that she was fine and when could they talk again? She needed to understand where the investigation into her brothers' deaths stood. He agreed to meet with her tomorrow. And then asked if Torin would be there?

Ashlynn sat back at the question. Would he be there? She had no doubt that he would if she asked. She hesitated to do that, reaching instead to scroll through her messages. She paused at the last one and a soft smile lit her face. Torin! He had reached out to her, simply stating that he would see her tomorrow and what time did she want to meet with Frank? He wanted to be there.

The couch would be her bed that night, she decided. She was on edge, not feeling safe anywhere anymore. She just didn't. The last week had taken that confidence from her. She began to pray, seeking relief and peace. She sensed that this was far from over, whatever it was that she was going through. And then there were those things from her brothers and their wives. She had spoken with the investigator in her hometown the previous week. He had no answers. The lawyer was refusing to talk. That was frustrating, he said. He could go no further at present and he just didn't want the case to go cold.

Ashlynn didn't want that either. She snuggled down under her blanket, drawing it up around her neck. She stared across the room, not sure where she was going with her thoughts but instead of determining that, she slept, her sleep dreamless and deep.

Torin stared out his front window, watching the night sky. He was torn, he knew, wanting to stay awake and watch for Ashlynn, but knowing that he had to be in his own home. He didn't like that. He just wanted to keep her safe. He too began to petition God for her safety. They had talked, those two, over the last days, intermittent at times, but enough that they had begun to get to know one another. All Torin was sure of was that he didn't want to lose her. His parents and brother had been around but he could not tell them much about what happened. Not because he didn't want to or couldn't but just because he didn't know.

Chapter 10

Frank studied Ashlynn and then Torin, not quite sure what was up with them. He had been there before Torin arrived and had watched him search for Ashlynn and then head for her as soon as he saw her. He looked up for a moment before he nodded. They were becoming a couple, that he knew.

Brinn had been watching Frank before she and Chani approached him.

"Frank? What can you tell us? Anything at all?" Brinn was deeply worried about her aunt. "And who is that with her?" Brinn had not been there when Torin had arrived.

"Who?" Frank smiled, knowing what Brinn was asking but wanting to hear her express her thoughts.

"That man with Aunt Ash? Who is he?"

"Him? That is Torin Callahan. He's the man who disappeared a week before your aunt did. He's the one who was kept captive with her."

"He is?" Chani turned to study him, a frown on her face as she watched her aunt interact with him. "What do we know about him?"

"Relax, Chani. He's friends with Adam. He's okay. And it looks as if your aunt is interested in him and he in her." Frank walked away at that point, heading for Ashlynn.

—

"Chani? Is that right?" Brinn searched for Darbi, beckoning her over. "Darbi, do you know Torin?"

Darbi nodded, not sure why Brinn was asking that.

"I do. We've worked together on a committee at church. I thought you knew that. Why the question?" Darbi stared at her cousin and then her sister.

"Watch Aunt Ash, Darbi. She's acting differently, isn't she?"

Darbi eyed her aunt, not quite sure what Brinn was saying. She simply shrugged. If Ashlynn wanted to tell them something, then she would. Until then, they wouldn't pry.

Torin watched the ladies' interaction over the evening. He nodded. He could see the love between them and how they watched out for one another. He also watched as they left before he approached Ashlynn. He wrapped her into a hug, a prayer whispering in her ear.

"Ashlynn? I want to ask something but I'm not sure how to. And that is not me." Torin studied her face, which she had tilted to look up at him. "Will you go out for a meal with me?"

"Torin? You mean that?" At his nod, she blinked for a moment, not quite sure where they were heading but this was changing where they were going in their friendship. "Sure. I guess. When?"

—

"Tomorrow? It is Saturday. We need to do something to try and get rid of what we're feeling about what happened."

"We do. I'm just not sure that a meal will do it, but we can try."

Ashlynn locked the door behind him, leaning back on it. She could hear her phone chiming and ignored it. She headed instead to her bedroom, to search through her clothes to find something that would do for the next day. She hadn't been on a date in years, she knew, and had no way of knowing how to act or what to say. *God, is this You? Did You bring Torin into my life? Is he my knight?*

Frank headed home, needing that break. He would be due back in court the next day, unfortunately, and he always hated that. He prayed that the culprit would take a plea deal. The man really didn't have a choice in his sentencing. He was guilty and everyone knew it.

Setting his shoes into the closet, he stretched. He could hear Sue in the living room, her voice showing that she was on a call. He headed for the kitchen, desperate for a cup of coffee. He smiled as he saw the pot waiting for him. Setting his phone on the counter, he scrolled through his messages, his finger stopping as he read one message. Emma had been busy, he noted, and would check his emails in the morning. Tonight, he just needed to relax. Frank turned as he felt Sue's hand on his back and simply hugged her.

"Okay, sweetheart?" Sue hugged him tighter, feeling the tension in him.

"I'll get there. Are you seeing Ashlynn this weekend?"

"We had planned to, but she's called. We talked instead." Sue hesitated for a moment. "She said that Torin asked her out for a meal tomorrow."

"He did? It doesn't surprise me. There's a chemistry there between them. And not just from what they went through. They'd be good for one another."

"They would be. I know Heather quite well from our ladies' Bible study. We've spent time talking. Torin is a good man."

"He is. I still have to talk with them about how they got home. They've given their statements but have adamantly refused to talk to me. I'll do that by Monday."

"I know you will. Now, you're not on call, are you?" Sue moved away, intent on fixing them something to eat.

"No, I'm not. Adam picked it up." He reached for their plates, giving Sue a kiss as he did so. "Now where?"

"The living room. That documentary we talked about is just about to start. I've been looking forward to it."

"The documentary it is then."

Flynn watched Darbi as she just sat on the couch before he moved to sit beside her and hug her.

"You're upset, love."

"I am. I talked with Eilis. She was really upset to hear what happened. She's heading for Aunt Ash's sometime tomorrow. Who did this, Flynn?"

"I have no idea, sweetheart. But someone is after your family. I would like to know why too."

"Does Aunt Ash know, do you think?"

Flynn shrugged.

"I don't know. She keeps a lot to herself, doesn't she? We need to respect that. We support her in what she does. And if that means that she starts dating Torin, then we support that. I have heard nothing but good about him. So I don't understand why he was abducted. Nor why your aunt was."

"Is it related to something here or to something in her past? And how were Dad and Uncle Adam involved? They still have not sorted out their murder."

"No, they haven't. All we can do is pray. God is here with each one of us. He was with us with what we went through. He's there for your aunt. He never allows anything that is not in His will."

"I get that. I just don't want Aunt Ash hurt anymore than she has been. She put her life on hold for us and did it willingly. I never heard her complain once about that. There would be a sad look on her face sometimes but she never said why."

"I'm sure that she has regrets. But I know your aunt well enough to know that she would not burden you ladies with anything like that."

Darbi's head went down against Flynn, content for the moment to be held.

———

"I fear for her, Flynn. This is far from over. I just wish I knew who it was. I would make them stop."

"And we will need to watch out for your four ladies. They'll go after you if they can't get to your aunt. That would hurt her worse than anything else."

The room grew quiet, both lost in their thoughts before Flynn began to pray out loud, petitioning God for their beloved aunt.

Chapter 11

The next morning, Ashlynn stared out her door window, fear coursing through her body. The man who had abducted her before was pacing on the city sidewalk, his eyes on her home. Her head went down against the door. She was so afraid that she could not even pray. Torin was due to arrive soon and she was so afraid that he would disappear again. Ashlynn no longer had any doubt that their kidnappers were one and the same. The only question was why. Well, that and another question as to how they were connected. They had talked and not found any connection between them that was obvious.

The man looked at the house once more, an evil grin on his face. He knew from experience that Ashlynn was terrified. It was one thing that he did well, terrorizing his victims. She would be back in his hands again, that he knew for sure. It was just a matter of waiting for his boss to give the go-ahead.

Ashlynn sank to the floor, her face buried in her hands. She was so afraid that she could not even pray. She knew it was at that time that the Holy Spirit would pray for her.

Her thoughts drifted back to that morning when she had awakened in Sam's cottage. She could remember Sam laughing as she had swiped Torin's coffee. He had not expected that, she knew, a smile briefly crossing her face.

___

Sam had fed them and then prayed with them. They had waited until mid-morning before Sam had pulled out his phone and handed it to Ashlynn.

"Call who you need to, Ashlynn. It's okay. Go ahead." Sam had stepped back, watching her closely. He could read her, he had decided, reading correctly how close to the edge that she was.

Ashlynn had stared at the phone and then up at Torin. Torin had simply sat beside her, swept her under an arm and waited. He knew that she was terrified. He was too. Only he had no idea why or who.

Ashlynn had stared at the phone once more after looking up at Torin and catching his nod. She sighed. This needed to be done. Only she didn't want to do that. She was just so afraid of bringing harm to her girls and their loved ones.

"Frank?" Ashlynn's voice had been hesitant at the abrupt manner with which Frank had answered his phone.

Frank stared at his phone for a moment. No, he decided, he didn't know that number, but it was Ashlynn's voice.

"Ashlynn? Is that you?" Frank was on his feet, heading for Adam, a hand tugging him back to Frank's office. He simply mouthed Ashlynn to Adam as they both sat.

"It is, Frank. I'm sorry. I don't know where I am. But I am safe. At least I think I am. I am with

Torin Callahan and a man named Sam. At Sam's cottage."

"I see. Are you heading home, Ashlynn?" Frank's eyes slid closed as he heard the subdued sob in Ashlynn's voice.

"We are, Frank. Where can we meet you? I think we need to speak with you."

"You do. How about at Jeff's? We can use his office without any problem." He waited as he heard Ashlynn speaking with someone.

"Sam said that's fine. Frank, I hate to ask but can you buy me some shoes? I don't have any." She thrust the phone at Torin as she buried her face against him, sobs shaking her for a moment.

"Frank? It's Torin. Yes, that's correct. She does not have any shoes. She said that she was taken from her kitchen and not allowed any footwear. It all happened too quickly." Torin listened for a moment, his eyes on his friend. "Sam? Yes, he'll bring us. And he'll talk with us. Where were we? At the Millar shack. Yes, Frank. That close to town. They moved us yesterday."

"We found where you were held, Torin, but were just too late I think to rescue you. We'll see you in about an hour then." Frank pocketed his phone, his eyes on Adam.

"They're safe?" Adam was incredulous for a moment.

"They are. I don't know that we'll get much information from them but we'll take what we can.

———

69

Torin has a friend bringing them back. I think I know who he is."

"And he's safe?" Adam was ready to fight for his friends.

"He is. He lives in another town but has worked closely with victims of crime over the years there and in this town. He'll be careful with them."

An hour later, Frank stood and watched as Ashlynn limped towards him. He shook his head, seeing the pain that she was trying to hide. *We'll need to get them both assessed, he decided. That would be the case for any victim. Lord, be with our friends. Heal them. And help us to solve this sooner than later, please.*

Ashlynn simply reached to hug Frank before hugging Adam, finding a seat in a nearby chair. She took with thanks the simple sneakers that Frank handed her, having guessed her preference.

"Okay, you two. What happened?" Frank pulled out his notebook and pen, his eyes on them.

Ashlynn and Torin shared a look before they both gave their stories. Frank sat back, a frown on his face. It didn't make sense that they had been moved, not in his mind. But there had to be a reason to take them out there. He knew the Millar shack and just how badly damaged it was. There would have been little shelter there for them.

"Okay, so we work with what you have given us. We'll set you up with police artists for sketches and then see what we can determine. Do you have any questions for us?"

Ashlynn shook her head and then paused.

"The girls?"

"They're fine, Ash. Just really worried about an aunt. Their fellows have tried to reassure them. Eilis is back tonight. I spoke with her. She called me after one of the others had called her."

"I hate this, you know. It wasn't supposed to happen to me. How does this relate to Adam and Aaron?" Ashlynn wasn't backing down from her questions, Frank knew her that well.

"We don't know yet, Ash. We're still working on that. I did speak with the investigator. He's surprised with what happened to you but then said we should have expected it. The ladies did receive other items of their parents, including a bracelet of yours."

"Mine? That is strange. Adam and Aaron would not have had that. All my jewelry was in my box." Ashlynn sighed, leaning against Torin. "Can we go now?"

"You can. Sam?"

"I'll see that they get home, Frank. If you need to talk with me, call me. You have my number."

"I do, and thank you, Sam. You've relieved our minds in some ways."

Frank watched as the trio walked away, Adam at his shoulder.

"Frank? This is strange. What are your thoughts?"

"My thoughts? Right now, they are so muddled, I'm not sure I could even begin to express what I think. But those two? It's not over for them. Not by a long shot."

"No, it isn't. That's the worry, isn't it? How do we protect them if we can't find out who is targeting them."

"I know. Emma was working on it as well as a friend of Ronan's. I'm sure his cousin and their other friends are working it as well."

Chapter 12

Ashlynn came back to the present as the doorbell chimed, startling her into a small scream. She could hear pounding at the door and her name being called. She knew that voice and scrambled to her feet. She flung open the door and then flung herself into Torin's arms, taking him by surprise. His arms tightened around her even as he nudged her back into the house and slammed the door behind him. The lock snapped shut before he just swept Ashlynn into his arms and carried her into the kitchen. He pulled back a chair with his foot and sat, simply holding her and praying for her.

Her heart settling down, Ashlynn just sat in Torin's arms. She finally looked up at him, finding him watching her.

"Ashlynn? Are you okay?" His worry for her was in his voice.

"No, I'm not. One of the men were out there. He was on the sidewalk, watching the house. I am so scared, Torin. And I don't scare."

"I know, my love. I know that. I didn't see anyone." He simply sat and held her for a moment, before he was on his feet, setting her back on the chair, and reaching to put on the kettle. "Let's have a cup of tea and then make some plans."

"What plans?" Ashlynn glared at him, so adorable, he thought, in a lady. She didn't seem to be

—

old enough to have raised the girls but he knew that she was.

"Plans for what we do. Have you security cameras?"

"I do. A friend named Joseph made sure that I had some installed when Brinn went through what she did." Ashlynn sighed. "How is this all related? Is there only one person after me or are there two, with someone after both of us?"

"I would say two, but it just doesn't seem that way. We need to think back to how we may have met before, other than our connection here."

"Maybe our parents? My brothers or their wives?" Ashlynn was on her feet, coming back from her office with pads of paper and coloured pens. "We need to think in colour, Torin. That may help."

"That's your work coming through." Torin knew that Ashlynn worked for a graphic designer, doing office work and simple designs. "Have you talked to your employer?"

"I talked to Gerry last night. I'm back to work on Monday. He'll make sure that I'm as safe as I can be. He needs me there or I would just take a leave of absence."

"No, you need to work. You need to keep yourself in as much of a routine as you can. I can make arrangements to drive you back and forth for now. I work from home a lot or my meetings are during the day. A lot of them I can do by conference call or video call. That's what we've been doing for the last couple of years."

"You have? Okay, I guess." Ashlynn's attention was on the paper in front of her as she began to list names and how she knew them. She took the cup of tea with thanks, not even realizing that Torin was standing watching her, his heart on his face.

Torin walked away, his phone out. He knew that he would not get Ashlynn out now for a meal, but that Jeff would gladly cater something for him and then deliver it himself. Jeff was a good friend who had done that before.

Ashlynn looked up, startled, when Torin's hand landed on her page. She frowned at him even as he grinned at her.

"Torin? I'm working."

"I know you are. Now, it's lunchtime. Jeff brought over a meal for us."

"He did? I didn't know that." Ashlynn was on her feet, shoving aside her paperwork for the moment. "What?" She glared at Torin as his hand stopped her.

"It's okay. I found your dishes and utensils. Sit, please, my love. We'll eat and then spend some time in prayer."

"I'm sorry. You wanted to take me out for a meal. I ruined that." Ashlynn was back in her chair, her face buried in her hands.

Torin sighed and then reached for her hands. He bit at his lip before he spoke, knowing that he would have to show a bit of his heart.

—

"Ashlynn, it's okay. It's not where we are that matters. It's time with you that matters. This is fine. We'll go out another day."

"Another day? Planning ahead, are you?" Ashlynn bit into her burger, her eyes closing as she savoured the taste. "This is so good. I don't know that anyone else makes burgers as good as Jeff does."

"I don't think anyone does." Torin wiped his mouth with a paper napkin. "Now, what have you discovered?"

"I am not sure what I have discovered. Here, you take a look at it. You may recognize some of the names." Ashlynn shoved the papers towards him.

Torin watched her instead, seeing how she was trying to hide her feelings from him.

"Don't hide your feelings, Ashlynn. We're in this together and we'll solve it together. Let's sort through this. When are we meeting with the girls and their fellows?"

"Tomorrow. I asked for that. We'll get together after church. We have been doing that as much as we can. I leave their weeks to them. They wanted to do this and I couldn't say no. I know at some point that will change." Ashlynn blinked back tears, knowing that she was now on her own and that scared her and saddened her.

Torin opened his mouth to speak and then snapped it closed. He didn't have the right to say anything, as much as he wanted to.

"Okay. Let's plan on that. Do you do the meal?"

Ashlynn nodded, glaring at the fridge.

"It's not the fridge's fault, Ashlynn." Torin laughed at the glare that she directed towards him. "We'll make do. I am sure the girls will help."

"They will. They already offered to do the meal this time." Ashlynn's gaze dropped back to the papers. "What have we discovered?"

"I'm not sure that we have." Torin's own gaze dropped down to the papers and he read through the names. He paused on a couple of names, his finger tapping the page. "These two. I have had run-ins with them in the past. How do you know them?"

Ashlynn's hand tilted his away from the paper.

"Them? Through work. Gerry has actually had both of them trespassed off the property. He refused to take their work and they became violent. It was scary. I haven't seen them for a while." She sighed. "We need to give this to Frank and Adam."

"We do. And that Emma you mentioned or Evan?"

Ashlynn nodded, searching for her phone. She snapped pictures of the papers and then sent them on.

"They'll work on them as they can." She sat back, watching him, liking that he was in her kitchen with her. He made her feel safe and cherished and loved, something that she had longed for all her life.

Torin looked up at that point, a softened look on his face. He simply touched her cheek and then looked back at the papers. He had conveyed so much in just that.

—

Chapter 13

Sunday morning found Ashlynn on her feet early in the morning. She wandered her home, just wanting to make sure that it was ready for her girls. She missed the daily contact with them but was glad for once that they were not there. She had seen evidence on the security camera that someone had been around her house during the night. That worried her.

Her phone chiming had her jumping and letting out a small scream. She searched for it, finding it in her office. She frowned as she didn't remember leaving it there. Shrugging, Ashlynn read her message. It was Torin, just to say good morning and could he drive her to church?

Is he for real, God? Is he really doing this? He doesn't have to. I mean, I know that he feels responsible for me, but he doesn't have to drive me places. It's like we're a couple of something.

A chime alerted her to a new message. It was Abe, just checking in, he said. What could they do for her, other than the obvious? He was deep in training that week but could free time if he needed to bring his security team that way. Or else Richard would be available or even Don.

She smiled. Her friends were looking out for her. She had had that all her life but it hadn't hit her as hard as it did that day, that her friends really did care about her. The next text caught her eye. It was Sue, just making sure that she was all right and asking if they could do lunch one day. Ashlynn needed that, Sue said. And yes, Frank would be around. He had promised Sue that he would be.

Torin watched Ashlynn carefully over the morning, his eyes searching the area around him. He could feel those eyes, the ones that were there anytime anyone had difficulty or danger. He felt her shifting closer to him over the service and noted the questioning looks that her nieces were sending her.

"Are you okay?" Torin finally bent his head after the service had concluded.

"I am. It's just that I feel watched." Ashlynn rubbed her hands together. "Is that normal?"

"It is, sweetheart. It is. It happens to everyone who goes through this." He stood, his hand reaching for hers, not seeing the questioning looks that the four younger ladies were exchanging.

Eilis was puzzled, not having seen the two together.

"Chani? What's going on with Aunt Ash?"

"That's right, you weren't here. I think they've become a couple." Chani shared a look with Ronan.

"They are? What do we know about him?"

"Adam is friends with him. He's single, never dating, until now. I would think that God has led the two of them together."

"Just like us." Eilis wrapped her hand around Declan's hand. "We're to have lunch with her, right?"

"We are. We've been working on what is going on. Tag is coming around later today. And Emma has been doing that." Chani sighed. "How do we help her? You know right well she'll tell us to stay away."

"She will, but we won't." Darbi walked away, her hand in Flynn's.

"Ashlynn?" Torin waited for her to turn towards him. "The girls are coming?"

"They should be. I don't know how to do this. It was different when it was the girls. Now it's me. I just worry that they'll be hurt."

"I know you are worrying. We are praying for this but it may be a while. Any more people around?"

Ashlynn shook her head, her eye on the clock. Torin had driven her home, waiting patiently for her to leave her seat in his car. He didn't rush her, sensing that she just needed that time, time to compose herself and get ready for any questions.

"Will they question you?" He grinned as she glared at him for a moment.

"They may and then again they may not. It depends." Ashlynn blinked rapidly for a moment, her thoughts muddled, not like her at all. She was usually organized in all ways.

"Then, let's go on it. I brought some fresh fruit for you."

"You didn't have to." Ashlynn's face lit up at his thoughtfulness.

"Yes, I did." He reached into his truck to pull out a box. Following her into the house, he set the box on the counter before he opened it. Turning, he held out a bouquet of yellow roses.

Ashlynn stared at him and then the roses.

"For me?" She could barely get the words out.

"For you, sweetheart. Here, take them and put them where you can see them." He turned back to the box, pulling out four more bouquets of mixed flowers. "And these are for your girls."

Ashlynn stared at him again before hugging him. She could hear the girls coming towards her and didn't care.

"Thank you, Torin. You don't know what that means for me."

"I think that I do. And these are not bribes. You have raised some beautiful young ladies. I was raised to bring flowers for any lady in the house. Today, that's you and your girls"

The four younger men shared a glance. This was not what they had expected but Ronan nodded. He had had a good talk with Adam the night before, just feeling him out about Torin. He liked what he had heard.

Flynn and Declan walked the backyard, neither one comfortable that Ashlynn was safe and by that, not comfortable that their ladies were safe when they were here. They could not find anything overtly obviously but they didn't think that they would.

Declan studied the house, a frown on his face.

"How bad do you think this is going to get?"

Flynn shrugged, not sure how to answer.

"Bad, I think. And it will draw in our ladies. They won't stay back, no matter what Ashlynn says."

"No, they won't. I just wonder who it is and how it all ties back to her brothers. That has to weigh on her mind, thinking for years it was an accident and then to find out it was murder."

"It has to. Darbi hasn't had much of an update recently, she said. She has been in touch with the investigator." Flynn sighed, knowing that they were still not free of the past and wanting it for her.

"Neither has Darbi. She's working away at trying to find the men or women involved but she doesn't know what to search for. She doesn't remember a lot from her past before her parents died."

"No, I don't think that she will. She was what, ten, when that happened? A friend told me that they have likely buried a lot in their grief." Flynn pointed towards the house. "And Ashlynn wasn't there a lot from what she said."

"No, she wasn't. And I think it is all entwined somehow. And our ladies are in danger. Only we don't know from whom or why." Declan walked back towards the house, leaving Flynn staring after him before he followed him.

Chapter 14

Ashlynn wandered her place of employment the next day, not sure what was wrong, but she strongly sensed that something was. Gerry watched her for a moment before he approached her. He had been in early, searching the building and outside. He had not liked what he had found. Reaching out to Frank, he had asked that someone come around as soon as they could.

"Ashlynn?" Gerry watched as she jumped and then spun to stare at him. He could tell that she was frightened. He just didn't know what he could do to relieve that.

"Gerry? Where did you come from? You're here early."

"I am, Ashlynn. I've been through the building and outside. Someone has managed to get in here and place those objects that you don't want to hear about. I spoke with Frank. He's coming around but for now he has sent a patrol officer to search. There will be a search team as well."

Ashlynn sighed, her head dropping for a moment.

"What am I to do, Gerry? I don't what to quit but I may have to. I can't put any of you at risk." Ashlynn stood uncertainly, her arms wrapped around herself, totally unlike her character.

Gerry nodded, knowing how Ashlynn would have felt about all this. He didn't need to ask her.

"We all understand that, Ashlynn. None of us want you to leave. You're an important part of our group. I have hired a security guard to be here during the day. That's not an issue at all." Gerry pointed towards the office that she usually used. "We've moved you to one of the offices near the back door. That way, if we have to get you out of here, we can. I talked to Richard and he was through."

Ashlynn stared at Gerry for a moment before she was past him and to the office where she had now been set up to work. She liked it better than the office where she had been.

"I like this, Gerry. I'll not be moving back to the other office." She smirked at him as he laughed.

"That's what we thought. That's not a problem." Gerry watched as Ashlynn sat at her desk, studying it and then looking around the room. "If you need anything, Ashlynn, there is a button under your desk. You press it? One of us come to here. It's linked to our computer system. You are not alone in this." Gerry hesitated for a moment and then walked away. He had had a long talk with Richard the previous week. Richard had been frank with him and what Ashlynn could face. He wanted to mitigate her danger at work as much as he could. If it came to it, he would send her home to work. Only, he knew that would never work. She would just refuse.

Ashlynn sighed once more before she started her work for the day. She felt as if she was behind, missing the last week, but her colleagues had picked up for her and had her up to date. That was the group that she worked with. She appreciated them all. She had been employed there since she graduated college, having intended to only stay for a while. The while just kept stretching out month by month.

Hearing a tap at her door, Ashlynn froze for a moment before she looked up. Gerry stood there, a grin on his face, a floral arrangement in his hands.

"Gerry? What did you do?" Ashlynn dropped her pen and rose, watching as he set down the flowers on her desk.

"I didn't. I don't know who they're from, but your niece did them."

"She did?" Ashlynn searched for a card, finding one. She was hesitant to open it but did at last. A smile crossed her face. "It's okay, Gerry. They're from Torin. Now, why would he do that?"

"Torin? He did this?" Gerry was surprised, knowing that Torin just didn't send flowers to ladies, other than to his mother. "They're beautiful and just right for a beautiful lady." He grinned at her as he walked away.

Ashlynn sank back into her chair, the card held in her hand. A softened look covered her face. Torin had done this, she thought, making her feel so special. She reached for her phone and send off a swift message just to thank him.

Torin felt his phone vibrate but had to ignore it. Frank sat across his desk from him, waiting to go back over what had happened. Torin didn't want to relive it but he didn't have much choice, he decided.

"Frank? Where do we stand with this? Have you found the men who abducted us?" Torin rubbed at his face, not sure what to think.

"No, we haven't. Unfortunately, we have to set it aside for now. There just isn't enough information to find them. We won't forget you two." Frank was angry that this was happening. He felt that Ashlynn had been through enough with her nieces. She didn't need this.

"I see. It's about what we expected. I have a team working on it as they can, but they state that they feel they are being blocked."

Frank stood and stared down at Torin before he nodded. He knew from Ronan that his cousin, Tag, and Tag's friends were working on it as was Emma. Only, no one seemed to be finding anything.

"We'll keep in touch with you both. Just take care when you're out and about. That's not a suggestion." Frank walked away, leaving Torin staring after him before he turned back to his work. He would have a busy day, he could see, and that meant that he couldn't slip away and take Ashlynn off to lunch.

That evening, Torin was finally able to reach for his phone. It had been a hectic day for some reason, totally unusual for him. He had arrived home at almost midnight and was exhausted. He and his staff had found someone trying to sabotage one of his projects and that had taken hours to resolve. He stopped for a

—

moment, his hand on the coffee carafe as a thought crossed his mind. Was this all related to Ashlynn? He needed to find out the names of her family. He could vaguely remember his parents talking about a family in her hometown where they had started a small business for someone. Were they connected there after all?

Torin scrolled through his messages, stopping at the one from Ashlynn. A soft smile crossed his face. Her flowers had arrived. He sent back a text to her, hearts attached without him thinking too much about it. She had his heart, he knew. He had never felt this way about a lady.

Ashlynn roused as she heard her phone. She had been receiving vague messages all evening, scaring her with their threat. She read Torin's message, a soft look crossing her face as well. She started at the hearts, wonder in her own heart. She was growing to love him as well. Did these mean he loved her?

Chapter 15

That weekend, the four young ladies approached their aunt, wanting to help her investigate what was going on. Only, they had no idea where to start.

"Aunt Ash?" Darbi hugged her. "Are you okay?"

Ashlynn turned, her eyes on Darbi for a moment.

"Am I okay? No, I don't think that I am. What are you four doing here?"

"We're here to start our investigation. Tag is heading our way, Ronan said." Chani reached to start a new pot of coffee. "They're meeting at our place and then heading here, if that's okay."

"You don't need to ask that." Ashlynn sighed as she heard the doorbell. "Now who!?'

"Aunt Ash?" Eilis was shocked at her aunt's reaction.

"This has been happening all week. The doorbell rings and there is no one there. And no, I don't open the door." Ashlynn headed that way, staring through the window before she opened the door. "Emma? What are you doing here? And Darci?"

"We're here to help. Abe and Doug have headed for Ronan's as that's where we understand the men are meeting. We're splitting forces as we say. And Joseph and Leah are here. Joseph's going over your office at your employer's request and then he's heading here. Leah is helping him, she says." Emma simply hugged

Ashlynn before she headed for where she could hear the younger ladies.

"Emma? You're here?" Brinn moved in on her, taking the box that she was handed. "Oh, great! You brought food from Rylee."

"We did. She insisted that we bring this. And Abe has some for the men. Now, were are we meeting?"

"The office. That way we have access to the computer." Darbi bit at her lip. "Can we solve this, Emma?"

"We will do the best that we can. And I understand that Tag's lady and her friends are heading this way?"

"That's what we hear." Eilis reached for a tray, loading it with the mugs and treats. "Can we solve this today?"

"Not likely totally but we'll do what we can." Emma moved with them, nodding at Darci as she stood with Ashlynn.

"Darci? Shouldn't we go with them?" Ashlynn was confused.

"We will. I just wanted to talk with you." Darci pulled back a chair, forcing Ashlynn to sit before she was in a chair beside her. "Talk to me. Tell me what's going on."

"I really don't know, Darci. I spent last night receiving vague messages on my phone. I sent them on to Frank but he's away for the weekend. And Adam is away as well."

"Send them to Jace at Emma's office. Joseph will be here in a bit. Show them to him. I know that Abe's team is wanting to work on this for you."

"I know." Ashlynn grew sober. "Isn't one of their ladies into family trees?"

"Kataleen is. She has asked for information from you. If you can give me that, then I'll pass it on. She'll research your family for you. You're thinking that somehow this goes back that far?"

"I do. We never resolved what was with the items the girls received. And then my bracelet was stolen from here and they received it with other items. This is so unnerving."

"It can be." Darci bit at her lip for a moment and then reached for a folder that she had set aside. "I did a profile for you, Ashlynn. I hope that it helps."

Ashlynn nodded, knowing that was what Darci did but only for friends. She had had a bad experience with a former police employer and had retired as a forensics psychologist.

"Here's a brief outline of it. Whoever it is? It goes back to your parents, I believe. She has watched you closely over the years. And yes, I believe that she had been the one responsible for your brothers' death. She is an evil, vindictive woman and has drawn in others of her family. She is a loner to some extent, mostly by her own choice. She is unmarried, has no children. She is avoided as much as people can. She is deep into crime and that may be why your brothers were killed. I can't tell you for sure until she is arrested and she has been interrogated."

"I see. So it does go back there. I am thinking that we need to go back there at some point. The investigator there is not getting too far. He says it's too old. I think that he's not trying too hard."

"That's what we're picking up, Ashlynn. Abe's brother-in-law, Gideon, and his former employer, Sidney, have picked this up and are investigating it. You do know that they are investigators."

Ashlynn sat back, a troubled look on her face.

"I want this over, Darci. I really don't care what it takes. The girls deserve answers. And we're not getting them."

"No, you're not. But don't do anything rash, Ashlynn. I know that's what you want to do but you can't. He's watching you closely, that's a given."

"He is. I have seen vehicles following me. I have seen the footsteps in the dew on the lawn where they have walked my yard. Torin says the same." Ashlynn paled, knowing that Torin was in danger. "Where does Torin come into this?"

"Torin? I have to speak with him. Where would I find him?"

Ashlynn had heard the door opening and then closing and footsteps heading their way. She simply smiled as Torin appeared and grinned at her.

"Right behind you, Darci. Torin has arrived. You talk with him and I'll go find the ladies." Ashlynn was on her feet, Torin reaching to hug her on the way by before he reached for her chair and sat.

Torin's eyes were on Darci. He had heard about her from the ladies but wasn't sure why she was there.

"You're Torin?" Darci spoke quietly, a frown on her face. She knew of him but had never met him.

"I am. And you are Darci?"

"I am." Darci's mouth snapped closed as she stared at Torin. A sudden rush of fear flooded her. He was in deep danger. Only she had no idea from who. She had not done a profile on his stalker and could feel the surge of impressions that always happened. "Torin? I need to do a profile on who's after you. Talk to me about what's going on."

Torin did just that. At one point, Darci had reached for a pad of paper and pen, jotting notes. Torin finally rose, heading for the ladies, seeing that Darci was deep into whatever or wherever it was that she had disappeared to. He stood, watching as the ladies worked away before he turned away. He glanced at the grandfather clock in the corner of the living room and nodded. That was what he could do, he decided, heading for the fridge and freezer. He could cook for them. It was almost lunchtime and they needed a break.

—

Chapter 16

That night, Ashlynn curled up on her couch, a cup of tea in her hand. She thought back over the day. A soft smile covered her face as she thought of Torin. He had simply been there, working in the background, just there in the background. Darci had left her profiles with them. Ashlynn had been surprised at the details that she had provided but Emma had simply smiled and hugged her, stating that was what Darci did. She had added that Darci's profiles were always accurate. Ashlynn had stared at her in shock, seeing the shock on her nieces' faces as well. They were not quite sure if they would believe Emma or not.

Torin turned from where he stood at the window. He had not left with the others, sending that Ashlynn didn't want to be alone. He would need to leave. He sat beside her, reaching for her hand, and bowing his head to pray for her. When he raised his head, he started at the lamp ornament on the wall.

"I like that lamp." He nodded towards it.

"You do? It's based on the wise virgins in the Bible. When I took on the care of the girls, those verses just kept repeating themselves in my head. I had them made just to remind us that we need to be wise and ready for anything."

"And you are." He rose, his hand reaching to pull her to her feet. "Come and lock up after me, love. It's getting late and has been a busy day for you."

—

Torin listened as she locked the doors before he looked up at the night sky. He thought that they had made progress that day but he was not certain of how much. He sighed as he moved towards his truck, stopping to stare at it for a moment before he climbed into it and drove home. He paced his home, his thoughts on Ashlynn. He wanted to protect her all day, every day, but couldn't. Torin finally admitted that he loved her but didn't think this was the time to tell her.

Sitting at his desk, Torin reached for his Bible. He needed to spend time in it, he knew. There was a crisis building for his lady. He wanted to be prepared to help her, if he could. Only he had no idea just how to do that. He had spoken with Abe, Doug, and Joseph that afternoon, just to get their perspective. He had been shocked when he heard their stories, not realizing what they had been through. He had taken notes, literally, he thought, and needed to read back through them. He also wanted to talk to the friends of Ronan's more, he decided. Just how he would do that, he wasn't sure, but he would.

Torin paused as he set his Bible aside. He had read through the verses on protection and help that he could find and spent time in communion with his Heavenly Father. He stared down at his watch. It was now early morning. He couldn't sleep, he knew, and rose, heading for the code pot and fresh coffee.

Hearing a noise outside, he paused, his hand reaching for the baseball bat that he had stashed by the backdoor. He didn't open it, just watched through the door window at the dark form that hesitated at the door and then left. He would wait until morning to open the door. He just wasn't ready to disappear again.

In the early morning hours, Torin opened the door and stared down at the package that sat there. This is what that person had been doing, he realized. He searched the area but didn't see anything or anyone that caused him concern. Reaching for the package, he straightened back up, staring at his name printed in block letters. He would need to talk to Frank or Adam, he thought, but not today. Today, he would set this aside. His lady had agreed to spend the day with him and his family, something that he was looking forward to. His parents had requested that. Ashlynn had hesitated when he asked, a grin on his face, before she had searched his face and then nodded.

Ashlynn turned that morning, her eyes on Torin as he approached her. His grin lit up his face and she smiled in response. She frowned to herself, though. Torin was beginning to be a big part of her life and that both excited her and scared her. *Lord, is this from You? Is he the knight that Mom and Dad prayed for before they left us too soon, when I was sixteen, dying within months of one another? If he is, please give me peace about our friendship.*

Torin turned after church towards Ashlynn, watching her react with her nieces. He knew that they loved one another and that worried him. He didn't want to come between them and that he was afraid was what would happen.

Troye watched his son closely, a frown on his own face. Torin was hurting, he knew, and undecided.

His eyes lifted to Ashlynn. He felt Heather's arm looped with his.

"He's in love, Troye." Her voice was soft

"He is, my dear, and not sure how to go about it. That is unusual for him." Troye turned them towards the door, walking back towards his car. "We can't help him out this time. It's something that he needs to work through for himself."

"It is. All we can is pray for them and support them. I intend to reach out to Ashlynn this week, just to see what I can do for her. She's on her own now, for the first time in years."

"She is. She was young to take on that responsibility. She never had a chance to be a single young lady. I know that he won't rush her." Troye pulled up to their garage and turned off the ignition. He sat for a moment, suddenly afraid for his oldest son and his lady. "I'm afraid for him, Heather."

"I am too. Who can we talk to?" Heather walked towards the house, waiting at Troye unlocked the door. She heard Tyrel's voice behind her as he called out a greeting.

"Mom? Dad? Is Torin here?" Tyrel greeted his mother with a kiss and a hug for his father

"Not yet. She was still with her nieces when we left church. How was the chapel?"

Tyrel's face lit up.

"It was great. It's always good to work with the ones down town. Although, one of the youths did come to me and I need to talk with Troye."

"Wait for now, son. We want today to be a time when they can forget for a while." Troye was reaching for the food that Heather had left ready.

Torin stood for a moment watching his family, his arm around Ashlynn. He could feel her leaning against him, a smile on her face as she watched the interaction.

"You're happy, love." Torin's voice was audible only to Ashlynn.

"I am, Torin. I am. This is wonderful. I can't remember much about Mom and Dad. Both were so sick the last few years that they were alive."

"They have made you part of the family. I'm glad. I would like that." Torin had taken his eyes off Ashlynn and didn't see the look that she gave him.

"Torin? Do you mean that?" Ashlynn had to repeat her question before he looked down at her.

"Mean what?" His eyes came back to her face, a puzzled look on his.

"What you just said? About me being part of your family?"

"I do, my love. I do. We need to talk but not right now." Torin moved her forward to greet his family, his eyes drifting back to her again and again.

Ashlynn moved through the meal, not really aware of what was said or what she was eating. She studied Torin before turning to answer a question from Tyrel. She needed some space she knew, to think and pray through what he said but for now she was fine where she was.

—

Chapter 17

Torin paced his home office late that night. He was exhausted and needed to sleep before his full day of meetings on the next day. Yet, his mind kept going back to Ashlynn's question if he meant what he had said. He had, he admitted to himself, but he hadn't meant to say it as yet.

He stared down at the package, his hand resting on it. His name was scrawled in black lettering. Torin nodded to himself. He would open it and then deal with it.

He carefully slit the tape on the box flaps and then folded them back. He stared at the tissue paper covering whatever was there before he reached to remove it. His eyes widened as he stared down at what was in the package.

A golden lamp lay among the remaining tissue paper. He reached out a finger to touch it and then lifted it out. It was almost identical to the ornament that Ashlynn had on her wall. He searched the paper remaining in the box. There was nothing to identify where it had come from or who had sent it.

Setting the lamp on his desk, Torin sat in his desk chair and stared at it. His mind drifted to the verses in the Bible that talked of lamps and lights and knew that he would be starting a study on them. He looked forward to that.

Lifting his head at last, he stared at the clock. It was the time that he generally rose and spent time in

—

prayer. He sighed. This had been another night when he didn't get to bed but spent the night in communication with God.

Walking away from his office downtown late that afternoon, Torin hesitated for a moment, his eyes on Eilis' floral shop before he headed that way. With a bouquet of roses in hand, he ran for his truck, heading for Ashlynn. He followed her car without realizing it for a moment. A grin lit up his face as he saw her parking and then turning as she heard his truck parking.

A smile lit up her face as she watched him walking towards her, the bouquet extended out. She reached for it, a soft thank you said before he simply wrapped her into his arms, holding on a bit longer as he felt the fear in her.

"Have a good day, love?" He turned her towards the house, taking her keys to unlock the door.

"I did. Let me change and I'll be right back. The vases are over the fridge." Ashlynn shoved the roses back at him and almost ran for her bedroom. The door softly closed behind her. It had been a very stressful day work wise, but it was the continuing text messages that were scaring her. They were getting more vicious and she was getting more terrified with each one. She had sent them on to Frank, who had been in touch. He hoped to meet with her that night but doubted that he could. Was there any way that she could just stay safe? Ashlynn had given a brief grin at his plaintive request, knowing that he meant it, even if he had asked it in jest. She knew how he thought.

—

Pulling on a favourite light sweater, Ashlynn pulled her hair back into a ponytail. She felt loved and cherished that night, all because of Torin. She looked up for a moment, blinking away the tears that clouded her eyes. She needed her parents right then, to walk her through that. Not having them, she just wished for her older brothers. Aaron had taken her in when their parents had died and had played the role of oldest brother in a way that reminded her so much of their father. The deaths had left a huge gap in her life. She prayed daily that they would find out why, without anyone else dying. And Ashlynn was afraid that would happen.

Torin turned from the stove where he had been working on a meal for them. He hadn't had to do that, but he had. He loved to cook and decided that cooking for just himself was so old. He wanted Ashlynn in his life and home and her girls and their fellows in and out as well.

"Okay, love?" Torin studied her for a moment before he sighed. "How many messages?"

Ashlynn shook for a moment before she nodded.

"Too many. And more vicious with each one. What did I ever do to deserve this?" She reached for plates to set the table, a finger touching the peach roses set in the middle of the table.

"You did nothing, love. It's how Satan works. He comes at us and as his troubles with us are thwarted by God, then he comes harder and harder. This is where it does get very dangerous. I am so afraid that I will lose you. And I don't want to do that."

Ashlynn nodded, not looking at him for a moment.

Clearing away their meal, Torin had watched Ashlynn. She was quiet that night, almost too quiet. He sighed to himself. He need to get her to talk with him and wasn't quite sure how to do that. She had taken with mugs of coffee and headed for the back deck. He watched as she did that, a thought crossing his mind.

"Ashlynn?" Torin sat beside her, wrapping her into his arms.

"Torin? How do we do this? How do we go on the offensive?" Ashlynn was thinking through what they could do. "I'm tired of this. This has been going on for too long."

"It has been. It's been going on since your brothers were killed, hasn't it? This is where it ends. With you. And we need to do what we can to keep you safe. Only, I don't know how we do that."

"I don't know either." Ashlynn rested back against Torin without being aware that she had. "I want to end this soon, Torin. This has hung over our heads since I was twenty-one or so. Those girls missed out on their parents in their lives, just in the everyday stuff but in the important things as well. That shouldn't have happened."

"It shouldn't have, but God did allow it. I have a friend who says that God has plans and purposes for us that we don't know about."

"Murphy?"

“That’s right. You know him, don’t you?”

“We do. We’ve met all of Abe’s team and their wives. They have quite the stories.”

“They do. I always told them that I didn’t want to go through what they did.” Torin grinned as she smiled. “And it appears that we are.”

“We are.” Ashlynn looked up at him. “You’ve received something?”

“I have. And I am not quite sure what to make of it.” He pulled out his phone and searched for the picture. Saying nothing, he simply handed her his phone.

Ashlynn stared at the photo, a look of wonder on her face.

“Josh! Josh did this. He’s a friend from when I was a teen. He’s the one who made the lamps for the girls and me. He’s heard about you and did this. He always said that when I began to date seriously and found my knight, that he would forward a lamp to him. When did it come?”

“It was on my deck yesterday morning. I didn’t open it until last night. How would he have heard?”

Ashlynn shrugged.

“I have no idea. He’s friends with us all. He has been there over the years in subtle ways helping from the background. He was like that when we were teens. Josh looked out for us all.”

“Then, we need to take a trip back to your hometown and find him. I would like to thank him.”

“We can do that.”

They grew quiet, content to be with one another, the night sounds echoing around them. Torin rose at last, walking back to his truck, his eyes searching for the person who he could feel watching him.

—

Chapter 18

That next Saturday, Ashlynn stood on the sidewalk outside a cafe in her hometown. She knew that her girls and their fellows were around her somewhere. When they had heard of Torin's plans to bring Ashlynn back to her hometown, they had insisted that they needed to come with her. They had not been back in months and felt that they needed to, for closure for one thing.

The investigator, a man named Rodney, had agreed to meet them mid-morning. They had some time to look around first before meeting him. Ashlynn had sighed, not wanting to do that but knowing that it was necessary.

A voice calling out her name had her spinning, Torin's hand there to steady her. Ashlynn's face lit up as she reached to hug the man who slid to a stop in front of her.

"Josh? Where did you come from?" Ashlynn stood back, Torin's arm around her.

"I was heading for the cafe and saw the girls. I figured that you would be here. How are you?" Josh studied his friend closely before raising his eyes to study Torin.

The men realized that they did know one another through Torin's philanthropic activities in the town.

"Torin? How are you?" Josh reached to shake Torin's hand before looking around. "We need to get Ashlynn out of sight."

____

"I'm not hiding any more, Josh. We're going on the offensive now. We're taking back our lives."

Josh grinned at her, recognizing in the lady the teen girl who had been determined not to be beaten down by life.

"That's the spirit, Ashlynn. Now, where do we go from here"

"First, thank you for the lamp." Torin simply stated his thanks. He looked around, seeing that the girls and their fellows had scattered.

"How be we walk then? There have been some changes." Josh pointed down the street.

"I can see that." Ashlynn's hand was tight in Torin's. "What else has happened here?"

"Well, let's see. You remember Ted Baker? He's been arrested and charged with a whole slew of crimes. It's been a long time coming."

"It has been." Ashlynn thought through the past. "I often wondered if he had anything to do with Aaron and Adam's deaths."

"We all do but he denies. Almost too much, we think." Josh hesitated as if he wanted to say something more

"And there's his family. His sister? I could see her doing something like that."

"So could I."

Torin had been listening to them speak before he looked around. He could feel the eyes on them that everyone always spoke about.

"How be we keep moving? Ashlynn is in danger by just standing still. What time are we meeting with the investigator?"

"Around 1, I think he said. We'll meet at the park in the centre of town. He feels that is safe enough." Ashlynn moved forward, eyeing the changes in her hometown. "So much has changed even in the last five years. I almost don't recognize this town anymore."

"I am sure that it has. Our council has become very proactive, drawing in new businesses. There are a lot of tourists now."

"That is new, isn't it? I think that once I leave here after this is all solved, I not likely will come back." Ashlynn was saddened at that but knew it to be the truth. She had no reason to do that, other than the graves of her family.

"I can see that." Josh walked with them for a time before he had to excuse himself. He just grinned at Torin's thanks, shrugging it off. He just didn't say how he had gotten it to Torin.

"Josh won't tell you how he got it to you." Ashlynn grinned at Torin for a moment. "He never does."

"I know. I just wish I could thank him in a tangible way." Torin pointed towards a vendor and purchased them a hot drink and muffins. "It's almost time to meet up with the girls, isn't it?"

"They're there already." Ashlynn pointed to the gazebo. "They're waiting for us. And Rodney seems to be there as well."

"Before we go there, let me pray for you. This may well be life changing for you, Ashlynn, and we need to cover you with God's protection."

Ashlynn waited for his prayer before hugging him. Her hand in his, she walked towards the group waiting for her, not sure what they would be told. She only knew that she needed this and to hear what Rodney had to say.

Rodney stood as he watched Ashlynn approaching him. He had been friends with her brothers and had been devastated for her and the girls when they had been killed. He had worked the case on his own time until he had made detective and then taken a post on the cold case squad. This had been one case that had haunted them all on that squad. Ashlynn's family had been thought to be one of the founding members of the town and everyone wanted to solve this for the ladies.

"Rodney? How are you?" Ashlynn reached to hug him, remembering him from her teen years.

"I'm doing okay. And you?" He watched her with keen eyes before those eyes raised to study Torin. "Torin? I didn't know that you were here."

"Rodney? You're the detective? I had no idea that you were working on this." Torin reached to shake Rodney's hand. "How is the club doing?"

"It's doing great. We have an updated report going in to your office in the next couple of weeks. Your support has been much appreciated." Rodney studied the area around them. It was not his first choice for a place to meet but he had made arrangements to have officers around the perimeter, just in case.

"You are more than welcome. I know how hard it has been for the teens in this town. Your group has made a real difference in them. We are happy to help. If you need more funding, talk to Barnabas Carey of the Barnabas Foundation. He's always on the look out for causes that help others."

"I have been in touch, thank you. He's been wonderful to work with." Rodney watched as the younger ladies greeted their aunt, standing almost shoulder to shoulder with Torin. "Torin? What's going on here?"

"What's going on? You mean with me here?" At Rodney's nod, Torin sighed. "I was kidnapped, held for a week, and then Ashlynn just appeared. No one asked us for anything or told us anything. We were finally able to escape, but someone has been targeting her since then. I would suspect it's been going on since her first niece went through what she did."

"We know it does. Frank has kept me updated as to what has been happening and what they have received. It doesn't make a lot of sense."

"No, it doesn't. It's scaring Ashlynn and her girls. Their fellows want to solve it and are working with friends to do so. We just seem to be missing one piece of information that we need to do that." Torin was frustrated, that much was obvious.

"I understand that. With these cases? It only takes a small piece of information to solve it. With the arrest of Ted Baker, people are starting to talk to some degree. We had no idea how much he had been involved in."

"I'm sure that you didn't. I have found from experience that they hide and hide well."

"They can do that. It makes for a lot more work for us but we are determined to solve this and soon. They deserve it." Rodney moved to sit near Ashlynn, leaving Torin watching her before he sat beside her, his arm around her.

Chapter 19

Ashlynn watched her nieces closely. This would change what they knew, she thought, and what they felt. Rodney would not have agreed to meet with them unless he had information for them. She could tell that he was ready to talk with them but was letting them have time to adjust what they were thinking. She lifted her eyes, seeing uniformed officers walking around the park but she also saw a man staring at their group. Ashlynn didn't think that she knew him but he seemed to know her.

"Ashlynn? We can share some information with you. But there is a number of leads that we are following. Those leads do tie back to your family. I'm sorry that we have taken this long to try and solve it for you."

"It's okay, Rodney. It's in God's timing. We want to rush and solve things, but God has a reason for this taking so long. Aaron and Adam would be the first to tell you that." Ashlynn reached for Torin's hand, needing to feel his hand on hers.

"Thank you for that, Ashlynn. Ladies? I understand that each of you have received something of your parents. From what we have determined, Aaron and Adam were targeted by Ted Baker. The reason why? That's what we are still working to determine. It is not from anything that they did. It seems to be more revenge. What that revenge is for? We don't know." Rodney studied Ashlynn, seeing the frown on her face. "Ashlynn?"

Ashlynn shook her head, her eyes on Brinn. Brinn was frowning at her aunt.

"Aunt Ash? What did you remember?"

"Nothing really, Brinn. There just doesn't seem to be anything that I can remember. And I wish that I could. Your fathers, girls, kept their business life away from you and your mothers. They told me that when they came home, business was left at the office. That their time at home was to be with you and your moms. They included me in that as well once Mom and Dad died."

"Your parents died from natural causes, Ashlynn, if I remember correctly?"

"They did. Mom developed kidney disease and was waiting for a transplant. That didn't happen in time. Dad had heart disease. We think that he died from a broken heart. He didn't live much past Mom." Ashlynn wiped at her eyes, taking with a soft word of thanks the handkerchief that Torin handed her.

"That's what I thought I remembered. I am so sorry, Ashlynn. You were too young to lose them." Rodney stared down at the ground for a moment. "Frank has been in touch for the last while, trying to work with me on this. We have made progress. Ted Baker was involved to some degree but we're not sure how much. His wife has left town. She left about the time that this all started. She has agreed to speak with us now that he is under arrest. His sister has disappeared. We have evidence that she has been involved in his crime activities as has her husband."

"His sister? Isn't she a lawyer?" Ashlynn paled. "She was friends with the lawyer who was supposed to be the one taking care of the estates. Only the will changed that. That lawyer was removed but it was after items disappeared from the house. We put it down to thefts from outsiders. Has he been the one?"

"That's the word that we have. We searched his house when he was arrested. We can't comment on what we found but there is evidence that your family is not the only one that he targeted. He is up before the law society now and has lost his license to practice. In fact, that happened well over a year ago." Rodney stopped at the look on Chani's face. "Chani?"

"That was before this all started? Did he blame us for that?" Chani reached for Eilis' hand.

"That would make sense." Darbi nodded at Rodney. "If he thought that we were responsible for that, then he would come after us and try to destroy us."

"That's what we are thinking, Darbi. But there are many others whom he took advantage of. He is facing multiple law suits and has been for a number of years. He's been delaying them as much as he can. And he can't find a lawyer to represent him."

"A dead cause, is what you're saying?" Gareth nodded in turn. "That's what Dad has come up with." He handed over a sealed envelope that he had been carrying. "This is what Dad has found. He's an investigator and has been working on this since Brinn and I went through what we did."

"He has? I know of your dad, Gareth. He's thorough and doesn't say anything unless is proven. And yes, Emma has been in touch. I have no idea how she found my name."

"Frank." Ashlynn smiled for a moment. "He would have spoken with her, just to see what she could come up with. And she will come up with what you need. That's what she does best."

"She does. Now, how do we keep you safe, Ashlynn? They haven't gone after your girls yet, but they may do that to get to you."

"That's what we're afraid of." Ashlynn drew in a shuddering breath, her gaze returning to the man watching her. "Rodney, there's a man watching us. I don't know him but he seems interested in what we're talking about."

"There is?" Rodney's phone was out and he spoke quietly into it. "He'll be taken into custody, Ashlynn." He pocketed his phone, watching her reaction to the man's arrest. "He'll be questioned. Now, when are you heading back home?"

"Shortly, I think." Ashlynn leaned against Torin, suddenly exhausted. "This is draining, Rodney. How do you do what you are doing?"

"We do it because we have to. We do it because of people like you. People who we want to help find the answers and closure to what their families are going through. And we will find those answers." He stayed for a while longer, just chatting in general before he rose, a prayer on his lips as he walked away.

He had to interview the man arrested and doubted that he would get any answers.

Ashlynn watched her nieces closely, seeing how upset that they were but were trying hard to hide it. She sighed to herself, hearing Torin's whispered prayer in her ear. She was thankful that he was in her life. She wasn't sure how she could manage this without him.

"You okay?" Torin's voice was low, just loud enough for her to hear him.

She shrugged.

"I'm not sure, any more, how to feel. This changes it, doesn't it?" She tilted her head to look up at him.

"Not really. We just know who is involved."

"We know one of the people. We don't know if there is someone behind him or who he has hired to work for him."

Torin watched as Ronan had turned as Ashlynn spoke. "Ronan?"

"That's what we can't figure out, Torin. Who all is involved?" Ronan looked around at the group. "I mean, we now know one of the figures, but not who else, just as you said. And how do we do that? We're finding ourselves watched and followed, particularly if we're heading towards Ashlynn's home. We need to keep ourselves safe but we don't want to avoid contact with her."

"That's what we thought, Ronan." Ashlynn leaned forward, her hands clasped together. "We need to make plans. We will not let whoever this is destroy our family. And I think that is what they want. If they drive a wedge between us, then they have won."

Flynn nodded, his eyes on Darbi.

"Darbi and I spoke about that last night. What would have happened to the girls if you had not taken them in, Ashlynn?" Flynn watched as Ashlynn's face paled.

"They would have gone into foster care of some kind and likely been separated. That would have destroyed our family." Her hands came up to cover her face as her emotions got the best of her for the moment.

"That's it exactly, Aunt Ash." Chani spoke up, rising to come and wrap her aunt into a hug. "If we hadn't been together, we would not have had the relationship with one another that we did. Our family would have been destroyed. I just don't understand why."

"There has to be something in your history that has led to this. We'll look into it more." Torin shared a look with the other four men. "For now, let's spend some time in prayer before we find somewhere we can grab a meal. We need to set this aside for the rest of the day. It will continue to prey on us and wear us down to the point that we're vulnerable."

Chapter 20

Ashlynn paced her office at work, waiting for her program to work through the changes that had been necessary. She spun to stare at the monitor. No, it wasn't ready yet, she thought. She grabbed her mug to head for the kitchen area, hoping that someone had made a fresh pot. And they had, she thought. She could hear conversation and laughter from her colleagues. It was a small office, only five employees as well as Gerry. She had been one of the first that he had hired, right out of college. He had also supported her as she took on the care of her nieces, gracious with the time off that she needed. Her colleagues had supported her as well. None of them had ever left for other work, and that said something about Gerry and the work environment.

Gerry stood for a moment, staring down at the sheaf of papers in his hand.

"Ashlynn, you're working on the Waters' project?"

"I was. I finished it off yesterday. Why?" Ashlynn turned to face him, a question on her face.

"Because they have decided that they want changes. This is not making sense." Gerry handed her the paperwork.

Ashlynn frowned as she stared down at the paperwork.

____

"This isn't from them. I don't recognize that email address. And that's not their phone number. Someone is trying to harm your business."

"They are, aren't they?" Gerry frowned at her once more. "Okay, so I'll call them."

"Wait, Gerry. I have an email from them. It came this morning." Ashlynn was past him and to her office, pulling up her email program. She pointed. "Here. This is from this morning. They have approved it."

Gerry sighed. This was bizarre, he thought.

"Okay. I'll pass this on to Frank."

"Gerry, pass it on to Micah at Abe's. He'll look into it for you."

"He will? Of course he will. Thank you, Ashlynn." Gerry disappeared, leaving Ashlynn to shake her head before she was deep into her work again.

Moving through her house that night, Ashlynn felt something off. She turned to her computer and brought up her security program. It was as she thought. Someone had been in her home. Only the security system had not alerted her. She didn't recognize the person.

"Frank? It's Ashlynn. Are you working tonight?" Ashlynn almost held her breath waiting for his response.

"I am, Ash. What's going on?"

"Someone has gotten into my house and past the security system. They should not have been able to do that. Joseph set it really strong and my password is one no one would ever think of." Ashlynn paced her home, an arm wrapped around herself. She was ready to run, only that would not solve anything.

Frank gestured to Adam, turning from the murder scene that they had just worked. Adam ran his way, not sure what was going on.

"Frank?"

"In the car, Adam. Ashlynn just called. Someone has been through her home." Frank flicked on his lights and siren and headed away.

"In her home? How on earth?" Adam was shocked at that.

"Whoever it was got by her security system. That should not have happened." Frank pulled up to Ashlynn's house, finding her on the driveway. "Ashlynn?"

"In there, Frank. I could hear someone speaking, threatening me. I couldn't stay there." Ashlynn's face was white and she was shaking.

"In my car. Adam?" Frank's weapon was out even as Adam moved Ashlynn to the safety of the police car.

"The doors are locked, Ashlynn. We'll be right back." Adam's phone was out as he called in for help, even as his feet took him towards the house.

The two men moved through carefully, not finding anyone there, but hearing the voice.

———

"Where is it coming from?" Adam looked around, searching for the access to the attic. "We searched up there, I know."

"We did, but we need to do it again." Frank watched as Adam pulled down the folding ladder and was up it to enter the attic. He could hear him moving away before his head appeared once more.

"I found out how they got in. There is access to the garage from here. And there is motion sensors up here. This was done in the last couple of days."

"When Ashlynn was out of town. They would have had time to do that then." Frank holstered his weapon and turned as he heard footsteps moving his way. "We need to search the garage, fellows, and then the yard. The house has been accessed through the garage."

Adam dusted off his jeans and straightened up once more.

"I thought that we had the garage secured as well."

"We did. There has to be a way that they got in without setting off the sensors." Frank's phone was out as he dialled Joseph's number. Able to only leave a voice mail, Frank quickly did so, simply leaving a message for Joseph to call him. He had a question about Ashlynn's security system. Would he get back to him as soon as he could?

Frank walked towards his vehicle thirty minutes later, his eyes on his phone. What had been found was disturbing to say the least. Numerous motion sensors had been found, set to trigger taped voices when Ashlynn moved through her home. The techs had found the entry point, a hidden hatch to the outside that no one had ever known about.

"Frank?" Ashlynn was out of the car, standing in front of him, worry and fear on her face.

"Ashlynn? Did you know that you have a hidden hatch to your attic that is accessible from outside?" Frank watched her as her face paled even more and his hand went out to steady her.

"A hatch? To the attic? From outside?" Her voice rose as she spoke, ending in a squeak. "No, I didn't know that. I could have done without knowing that. Who could have known that?"

"That we don't know. We've secured it from the inside now so no one can get it. That's how they were able to get to the attic. And yes, there were motions sensors placed around. That set off voice recordings as you walked through the house. They were timed to start today."

"Today? Why today?" Ashlynn paced away from him and then spun, almost running to stand back in front of Frank, her eyes wide with shock. "Frank? It's Dad's birthday today. Why? Who would do this?"

Chapter 21

Frank shook his head an hour later. Torin had shown up and taken Ashlynn to his home. He had reached out to her girls and they had agreed to meet them there. Frank wasn't sure just what this was about. Adam stood near his car, waiting for him, his eyes searching the area. There were still patrol officers around, kept there for the time being.

A sudden yell from Adam had Frank spinning around, his eyes searching the area. Adam was running towards a man standing on the opposite sidewalk, a patrol officer moving in from that area. The man was tackled before he could disappear. Hauled to his feet and handcuffed, Adam nodded at the patrol officer, who moved off with the man.

Frank approached Adam, a puzzled look on his face.

"Adam. What was that all about?"

"He was watching the house. I recognized his photo from his mug shot. He's someone that we've been looking for. I just don't get how he got here or why he was. I'm not sure that we can ever get him to talk." Adam pulled the car door closed behind him. "This is just so bizarre."

"It is. Ashlynn is shaken by this. She told me that they were back to her hometown on Saturday and met with Rodney."

"They did? He called me this morning but I haven't had a chance to speak with them. I wonder if they found out anything."

"They may have." Frank drove away from Ashlynn's home, heading for Torin's place. He parked in the driveway, suddenly exhausted. He sat, praying for his friend and for themselves as they tried desperately to solve what was going on. He had no answers.

Ashlynn approached the car, her arms wrapped around her waist. She wanted to know what all he had found. Only, she didn't think that she would.

"Ashlynn?" Frank stopped in front of her.

"Frank? What all did you find?" Ashlynn was turned back towards the house, Frank and Adam flanking her.

"In the house, Ashlynn. Someone is out here watching you. There was someone at your home as well. We have taken him into custody."

Ashlynn was shocked, simply staring at Frank before Torin wrapped her into his hug.

"Frank? What was that you said?"

"That we arrested someone watching Ashlynn's home. In the house, you two. There are people around here watching as well."

Adam nodded at Frank and disappeared from sight, searching for the men. He approached a man standing in a neighbour's yard. When the man could give no good reason for being there, Adam simply arrested him. He waited for a patrol officer to appear.

———

Frank turned as Adam entered, simply handing him a plate of food. It was suppertime and they needed to eat. Ashlynn was not happy, he could tell, and he didn't blame her one bit. The younger ladies and their fellows had appeared, shock on their faces at the events that had transpired.

Darbi approached him, a question on her face. Chani followed her.

"Frank? Did you really arrest someone?"

"We did. We have no information yet that we can pass on. Once we do, then we will speak with you."

"But what about the new hatch in the house? Has it always been there?" Chani was puzzled.

"There was. It has been there all along, we suspect. It was well hidden but someone had found it out and used it."

"How long have they been doing this?" Brinn had appeared.

"That we don't know, Brinn. We can't tell. But we have modified the hatch so that they can't access it again. We have searched the attic and not found another hatch." Frank was watching Ashlynn as he spoke, knowing that she was terrified.

"Frank, what can we do?" Ashlynn's eyes were on her nieces, knowing that it was becoming more dangerous for them all.

"It is very dangerous now, Ashlynn. We have talked this over. This is where you need to be very vigilant now. All of you. We can't emphasize that enough. They will try and get you through the girls, Ashlynn. We all know that.”

Frank walked away an hour later, Adam at his side.

“They’re going to go on the offensive, Frank.” Adam’s voice was quiet.

“They are. And we can’t stop them. All we can do is give them as much information as we can.”

Ashlynn leaned into Torin’s hug, finding safety and security there. He had become so important to her. She just didn’t want to see him hurt.

“Ashlynn? Where do we go from here?” Torin’s heart was in his voice as he spoke.

“I don’t know, Torin. I just don’t know. This scares me more than anything. I am so afraid that one of the girls will be hurt.”

“And they may be. We’ll do our best to keep them safe. I spoke with Richard earlier today. He dropped into the office.”

“He did? And what did he have to say? I’m not leaving my home.”

“No, that won’t work. They would just follow you, whoever these men are. I think it goes back to the founding of your town.”

“You do? That’s what I think. I just wish I knew who I could speak with to determine that.”

“I know. I’ve been trying to come up with someone and can’t.” Torin’s arm was around her as he walked her to her door.

———

Ashlynn unlocked the door and then stood, staring into the house.

"Not wanting to go in?" Torin's voice was low and caring. He wouldn't want to enter the house either, if it had been him.

"No, I don't. And I need to." Ashlynn took a tentative step into the house and then stopped. "I can't do this, Torin." Her voice was filled with sobs.

"No, you can't. How be you pack a bag and I take you to Mom? She'll welcome you there."

"But I would be putting them in danger." She looked up at him, hope on her face.

"Not really. Their security system is one of the very best that you can find. No one gets in. She found out earlier what had happened when I was talking with Dad and asked that. It's either that or we find somewhere to get a license and get married tonight." He stared down at her, his heart on his face.

"Torin? Just what are you saying?" Ashlynn was in shock.

"That I love you and would marry you in a heartbeat if you would have me." Torin sighed. "This is not how I planned this. I wanted a romantic dinner, a walk, and then down on one knee to ask you."

"Torin? I don't need that. I can see your love for me all the time. And yes, I love you too. But we can't do that tonight. So, I guess it's your mom's."

"It is. I don't want to force you to do something that you don't want to."

"I know." Ashlynn reached to flick on lights before moving towards her bedroom. "Just give me a few minutes. I'll be right back."

Ashlynn almost floated to the bedroom, her thoughts muddled, totally unlike her. She was loved and loved in routine. Given that she was now in her thirties, she had not expected that at all. She had resigned herself to living out her days in a solitary manner.

Chapter 22

Heather turned from the bedroom door later that night, shutting it quietly behind her. Torin had shown up with Ashlynn, the lady looking so lost and forlorn that all Heather could do was hug her. She knew that Ashlynn was missing her mother.

"Mom?" Torin watched from the hallway, worry evident on his face.

"She's heading for bed, son." Heather reached to hug her son. "She needs it. Right now, she's not feeling very safe. Not that I blame her."

"No, she's not safe. That much is evident. Only we don't know how to keep her safe."

"No, you're not going to be able to, son." Troye had approached from behind him. "We need to talk with Richard, I think, and find out what he would suggest."

"I talked to him earlier and he's agreed to meet with us tomorrow. He was in the office today for something else."

"Then, we meet with him. You'll be taking Ashlynn to work, I gather, in the morning?"

Torin nodded, knowing that he would have a fight on his hand to do that.

"Head for bed, son. Morning will be here before you know it."

His parents watched as Torin walked away, heading for his boyhood bedroom. He hesitated at Ashlynn's door, a prayer raising for her before he headed for his bed and sleep. He didn't think that he would sleep but his body had other plants. He slept, a deep refreshing sleep.

Ashlynn roused in the early morning, earlier than anyone else. She was up, showered and dressed, heading for the kitchen before she turned. She sighed. She needed to head for work, only she didn't have her car and that was a problem.

Troye watched her, a frown on his face. He had roused earlier than she had, worry on his mind for his son and his lady.

"Ashlynn?" His voice had her spinning in fear. "It's okay. I was up anyway. What time do you need to be at work?"

Ashlynn flushed with embarrassment and then glanced at the clock.

"In about thirty minutes. Only I don't have a car."

"That's okay. I'll get you there. Torin is still sleeping. That's unusual for him. He's needed it."

"He does. He's in danger just being around me."

"He doesn't care about that. He's worried about you. We all are." Troye reached for the coffee pot. "Here, let's get you a coffee to go and I'll take you to work."

Ashlynn nodded before she reached for the mug that Troye was handing her. She settled at her desk a while later, booting up her computer and searching through her emails for what needed to be done that day.

Looking up a couple of hours later, she stared at Richard as he sat down in front of her desk, a grin on his face.

"Richard? What are you doing here?" Ashlynn was not surprised to see him.

"You bring me here." Richard dropped a folder in front of her, a hand resting on it for a moment. "These are some plans for you and Torin that we pray we never had to put into place. Read through them. Pray over them. Then talk to Torin. He'll have a copy of the same as you do."

"Thank you, Richard. I know that this is a step that we need to consider. I was praying that we didn't have to."

"I know, Ashlynn. But you may need to. I talked to Frank this morning. He called me and let me know what they found in your home. He thinks that you will be safe there for now but we may be looking at moving you somewhere else."

Ashlynn nodded, a sober look on her face.

"I get that, Richard. I just want my girls to be safe. And none of us can guarantee that."

"I think we can. They'll use scare tactics to make you out what you are seeing and feeling. They won't harm the girls. They will threaten them to get to you. They will not harm them because that will make you come after them. And they do not want that. Not yet. Their plan is to continue to terrorize you and Torin."

"I know that, Richard. They have invaded my home. I'm not sure that I can ever live there again and feel safe, even if this is resolved." Ashlynn rubbed at her face, trying to control her emotions. She could hear the voices from the other workers and then Gerry responding. "Maybe I need to quit work."

"You may need to look at taking a leave of absence. Gerry is fine with that. He approached me as well." Richard gave a tight grin at her look. "We're looking out for you, Ashlynn. Don has headed for Torin. Abe is weighing in as well."

"And Ian is threatening to fly us somewhere, isn't he?"

Richard laughed at her disgruntled comment.

"He has suggested that but you are not ready for that. I don't know that you ever will be or that you would have time to do that."

"Somehow, I don't think so. We need to meet with everyone, including the fellows' families. They are all at risk somehow."

"They are. Torin has agreed to have everyone at his place tonight. And one of us will be driving you to your home and then there. That is not an option, Ashlynn."

Richard rose and left, not sure that Ashlynn would be agreeable to what they wanted her to do. He paused in the parking lot before walking towards Silver.

"Richard?" Silver could read her boss and saw his hesitancy.

"She's not sure if she's on board. We need to convince her of that." Richard stared into the distance, trying to come up with a plan that would work.

"I'll talk with her, Richard, and see what we can do. She's afraid, not for herself, but for her girls. She's not sure what to think any more."

"No, she's not." Richard walked away, leaving Silver to head for the building

Gerry paused as he saw Silver and nodded. Richard was at work, he thought. *That's what we need. Lord, please protect our Ashlynn. She's an important part of our lives. Let no harm come to her.*

Chapter 23

Silver waited for Ashlynn to unlock her house door that evening and turn off the alarm. She had just shaken her head when Ashlynn had looked at her in surprise when Silver stated that she was driving her home. That was not an option.

Silver walked through her house, making Ashlynn stand by the door until she returned. She grinned at Ashlynn.

"It's okay, Ashlynn. Your house is safe. Go on and take the shower that you want to. Get some clean clothes on and then come on back. I'll search for some food for us. I know that your fellow will be heading this way."

"And just how would you know that?" Ashlynn grinned as Silver smirked at her. She had begun to enjoy the friendship that Silver was offering her.

"Stephen told on him. He's bringing him over. And I hear Richard is heading this way as well."

"Of course, he is." Ashlynn walked away, listening to Silver's laughter. She sighed to herself. She needed to work on her attitude. Only she didn't want to do that.

Lord, forgive me. I know that they are doing this for my good, to keep me alive. Only I don't think that person wants me dead. Not yet, anyway. He wants me to suffer and just what that is? I have no idea.

———

Dressed in her comfortable jeans and favourite long-sleeved T-shirt, Ashlynn paused in the hallway, her head tilting. *Yes,* she thought, *they're here. How do I face Torin, after what he said?*

Torin was waiting for her, his arms open as she first stared at him and then ran for him. His arms tightened around her as she wept from fear and then relief. He was here and wanted her with him. That was all she could think of.

"Okay, love?" Torin turned her around, taking her back to the office and seating her on the love seat there.

"I am. Now." She looked up through tear-drenched eyes.

The tears broke his heart. He knew that she was showing her vulnerability to him, not something that she would do to just anyone. He didn't think that she had even done that to her nieces in all the years that she had raised them. Her breaking point had come, and it was up to him to rescue her and help her to heal.

"I meant what I said last night, love. I do love you and want to marry you. Only I'm not sure if you're ready for that." Torin held his breath for a moment as he watched her, his heart in his eyes.

Ashlynn studied him, read his heart, and nodded.

"I do love you, Torin. I would be honoured to be your wife."

Torin simply kissed her at that point. They would make plans but for now, it was enough that she was his and in his arms.

"We'll plan, love. We'll make plans."

"I don't want a long engagement, Torin. Not with what we're going through. We need to be together, for however long that God allows us." Ashlynn shifted as he did, watching as his hand reached for his shirt pocket.

Torin placed the ruby ring on her finger and then paused.

"We need to talk to our families first."

"We do. They're not here and they need to be." Ashlynn reluctantly pulled off the ring, placing it on the necklace around her neck. "I'll put it back tonight."

They rose, heading for the kitchen, hearing more voices that had been there. Ashlynn stopped in surprise. Her girls were there as were Torin's parents and brother. They looked at one another, not sure who had arranged that.

Richard approached them, sensing a change in them, but not sure what.

"We brought your families in, Ashlynn, Torin. We need to discuss our next moves and this involves them."

"It does. Thank you. We need to speak with them." Torin moved past him, greeting the girls and then his family.

Ashlynn watched his interaction with the girls and smiled. They were accepting him and that pleased her greatly. She had often wondered what it would be like if she had found someone and now she knew.

Heather stopped besides her, an arm around the younger lady.

"You two have come to a decision. I can tell." Heather hugged her tighter and then just stood. "I won't pry, Ashlynn. You will tell me when you are able to. That I know."

"We have, Heather. I am glad that you are all here. We do want to speak with you. We just didn't think that it would be tonight." Ashlynn's eyes found Tyrel who nodded.

Tyrel turned to his brother, finding him standing and staring out of a window, a puzzled look on his face.

"Torin? What's wrong?" Tyrel's hand rested on his brother's shoulder.

"I feel something moving in on us, Ty. I'm just not sure what or who. And that scares me."

"I know. I can feel it too. We need to figure it out."

"And we will. Listen, I need to talk with you, Mom and Dad, and Ashlynn's family and tonight. We just need to do it in private."

"Not a problem, Tor. Richard's group is leaving in about five minutes he said. We can talk then. Let's find our food and places to eat."

Richard watched Torin and then Ashlynn before he sighed. They were up to something, he knew. He just didn't know what it was.

Torin turned as the meal was cleaned up and the families had found seats in the living room. He drew

Ashlynn back to the kitchen, kissing her before hugging her.

"You can put your ring back on, love. We'll tell them tonight. Richard did what we wanted, without knowing that. We'll tell them and then start making plans. Right now, this is where we are."

"I know." Ashlynn's fingers trembled as she held the ring, feeling Torin take it from her and slip it back on her finger.

The families looked up as the couple approached, hand in hand, before they were on their feet. Nothing needed to be said, they knew. Torin and Ashlynn had made a decision, a decision to join their lives and marry.

Ashlynn watched her nieces interact with Torin. They loved him, she could tell, and he loved them. It had not taken long.

Tyrel stood beside her, an arm around her shoulder, just as her brothers would have done. She was grateful to have a brother in her life again. She was sad, though, that her own brothers could not be here to see this and that her parents weren't either.

"They know, Ashlynn. Your family knows. And they approve." He grinned at her as she stared up at him. "God allows them to know."

"I understand that, but it is still hard not having them here."

"We know. Listen, Mom will help you plan if you want that." Tyrel had been watching his mother, seeing her interacting with the younger men. His father was standing back, just watching them all, but Tyrel could see the worry in his eyes.

"Thank you, Tyrel. This helps." She hugged him and then made her way to Brinn, finding her oldest niece reaching for her. "Brinn?"

"I'm so happy for you, Aunt Ash. He is just who you need."

Chapter 24

Richard watched Frank for a moment before he slid into the booth across from him. He had tracked the detective down at Jeff's cafe, needing to speak with him.

Frank looked up, nodded and then continued with his meal. He had not had a chance to grab his breakfast and wanted to finish his lunch before he was called out to another crime scene.

"Richard?" Frank sat back, his plate pushed to one side, waiting for Richard to speak.

Richard sighed, wondering if Ashlynn had spoken with Frank.

"Have you talked with either Ashlynn or Torin today?"

"I spoke with Ashlynn. She's told me. Not what we wanted but it is her life." Frank sighed to himself. He just couldn't understand her reasoning.

"She's in love, Frank. She didn't think that she would ever have this opportunity. She told me once that she felt too old to find love, that no one would want her at her age."

Frank nodded. They had had a similar conversation at one point a few years ago.

"She has said that. And she is so wrong. She is a wonderful friend to Sue and has been for years. We've been praying for this for her. Only, I never expected it to happen when she was in danger."

Richard began to laugh at that, his hands cupped around his mug of coffee. Frank stared at him and then began to laugh as well.

"I know. Look at her nieces." Frank shook his head. "Torin is just who she needs and she is just who he needs."

"They are. Now, where do we stand?" Richard sobered, knowing that Ashlynn's danger was not over.

"Where do we stand? Right now, we don't have enough information to move forward. Anyone who we have arrested is not talking. We don't know who they have been employed by." Frank was frustrated with that.

"I see. We've spoken with both of them just last night. Their families were part of the discussion. We have set up guidelines with them and what they can expect going forward. If they marry soon, it might make it easier to protect them if they are in one house. But it makes it more difficult as they would be newlyweds and need their privacy."

"It's complicated, no matter what way we look at it." Frank pulled out his phone, a frown on his face. "Abe is in town and looking for us. Did you expect him?"

"No, I didn't but I would be glad to hear what he has to say."

Abe walked through the cafe, heading for the two men, sliding in beside Frank. Jeff set the mug of coffee he had asked for and then moved away. He was deeply troubled about Ashlynn, word on the street was that

———

someone wanted her and wanted her dead. He had reached out to Frank and mentioned that to him. Frank had nodded and asked for any details that Jeff knew.

Abe stirred at his coffee, not sure how to proceed. He slid the envelopes that he had been holding across the table to both Frank and Richard.

"Emma has been busy as has Kat and Darci. This contains what they have discovered. And it is what we discussed. It goes back to the founding of the town and does involve Torin's family as well. It is interesting reading as to the connection between the families."

"It is? Okay, we'll read through it. We'll reach out to the ladies if we have questions."

"Emma expects that as does Darci." Abe was on his feet and moving away from them. He needed to be back at his business, a team in for security training that needed his attention.

"If this helps, I'll be glad to have it." Richard reached for his envelope and rose. "Call me if you need me, Frank." He walked away, wanting to read through the information and then discuss it with his team.

Frank rose as well, walking thoughtfully through the town, his thoughts troubled. If Emma had found what she usually did, and he had no doubt that she had, it would make more work for him to prove it, but prove it he would.

Ashlynn turned from her desk, mid-afternoon, her work done for the day. She rose to find Gerry, standing in his office doorway for a moment before she approached to sit across from him

Gerry studied her before his attention went back to the emails he was working through. He sat back at last, exhausted, wishing that he could take that trip his wife wanted him to but understood that he wanted to wait.

"Ashlynn? You're troubled?"

"I am, Gerry, and I don't know why." Ashlynn rubbed at her face, her ring glinting in the light.

"You're troubled, Ashlynn, not sure what is going on. And you're missing your parents and brothers. You want to share your news with them and they're not here. You're making plans that you discussed with your mother when you were young and you want her to share those plans with you."

"That's it, Gerry. It's also the danger that we're in. I am afraid that I will lose Torin to this."

"And that's a legitimate concern. What can we do to help you?" Gerry leaned forward, his arms resting on the desktop.

"I'm not sure any more, Gerry. I need to keep working but I'm being followed coming here, when I go out during the day, and then back home. I'm afraid that someone here will get hurt."

"We get that, Ashlynn. We know the risks and are willing to work with you on them." Gerry rose, coming around to draw her to her feet. "Head on home, Ashlynn. You'll all caught up. Take tomorrow off, it's Friday. Work on those wedding plans."

Ashlynn reached to hug him and walked away. Gerry sighed and then began to pray for his friend and employee. This was not over for her, he knew.

Ashlynn walked away that day, heading for the downtown area. She searched the shops, not finding what she wanted. She sighed, returned to her car, and drove home. She was frustrated, Ashlynn knew, and didn't know how to resolve the problem.

Heather's text caught her by surprise. Did Ashlynn want her to go shopping with her? She had reached out to Sue and they would be available tomorrow, if she wanted to. Or did she want to wait for Saturday and have the girls with them?"

Ashlynn's face lit up. She knew that the girls were all off for various reasons the next day. She sent out a group text, accepting the offer. The responses were quick and positive. She felt the faint stirrings of excitement beginning.

Mom, I wish you were here, but you have sent ladies to stand in for you. Thank you, Lord, for that. I need them. Tell my mom how much I love her.

Chapter 25

Ashlynn walked towards Heather and Sue the next morning, the four nieces flanking her. Their excited chatter had brought a smile to her face and lightness to her step. The girls had been excited, trying hard to plan her wedding despite her protests. She had let them talk and chatter away and then sat back, her thoughts on Torin and what their discussion had been.

Heather reached to hug Ashlynn, holding on for a bit longer than normal. She knew that Ashlynn was hurting in so many ways. Sue reached to hug her friend, a prayer whispered in her ear.

"Okay, Ashlynn. We're here. Now, what are you thinking?" Heather reached to open the bridal shop door, waving the other ladies through.

"I haven't really thought of what I want. Simple, I think. I like the idea of a tea-length dress."

"That's so you, Aunt Ash." Eilis waved at the shop owner, a friend from school. "Let's see what we can find."

There was a lot of laughter and tears that morning. Ashlynn stood at last in front of a mirror, her eyes on her dress, critically turning here and there. It was perfect, she decided, just what she wanted.

"What about a veil, Aunt Ash?" Chani stood to one side, watching her aunt.

"No veil, I think, Chani. That's not me. I have Mom's gold hair clip. I'll use that. Torin wants me to leave my hair down." She looked around with a glint of mischief. "Eilis? Has he talked to you yet?"

Eilis began to laugh. Torin had shown up in her shop the day before, ordering flowers.

"He was there yesterday. Now, who is your attendant?"

"You four girls are. Brinn, you're the matron of honour, as the oldest. I can't do this without you four being part of it. There will be danger, I know, but Richard has agreed to make it safe for us. We talked with the pastor last night." Ashlynn turned to face them, her hands on the lace covered dress. "This is the dress, I think, girls. Now, about you four?"

"We have dresses that we can wear, Aunt Ash. That way, we don't have that expense." Darbi reached to hug her aunt, her emotions mixed. "This is hard, you know. You've always been there for us. Now, we're going separate ways, it seems, and starting our own lives without you being there all the time."

"It's only right that you do. You can't live with me forever. This is God's plan for you. Now, let me get this off and then we'll do lunch. Heather? Sue? Do you have time?"

"We do, Ashlynn." Heather hesitated for a moment. "I have no idea what your plans include for a meal, but Troye and I would like to look after that for you."

"You would?" Ashlynn had changed back to her jeans and sweater. "Then, thank you. We were

144

thinking more along the lines of a tea rather than a full meal. That would keep the time around us down."

"It will. But know this. You will be protected that day. We'll make sure of that." Sue had already spoken with Richard and Frank, getting their assurance on that.

"Thank you."

Torin watched as Ashlynn walked towards him, a smile lighting his face. He had appeared at her home in the afternoon, anxious to hear how her day had been. They had obtained their marriage license the day before. Now all that mattered was to set a date. Torin was afraid for his lady and that was no lie.

"Torin!" Ashlynn ran towards him, being swept into his arms and spun in a circle. "You're here already. Did you play hooky from work?"

"I did, love. I did. I wanted to see how your day went. Mom wouldn't say, just said to ask you." He laughed as she swatted at him.

"It went well. I found my dress. The girls are all set. Your mom said that she and your dad will take care of the meal. What do we have left to do?"

"Set a date. How about next Saturday?" He smiled as she gaped at him before her mouth snapped closed.

"Next Saturday? Let me see. I need to check my social calendar to make sure that I don't have an important date." Ashlynn grinned at him mischievously until he just kissed her. "Next Saturday works."

"Thank you, love." Torin turned her to the house. "Let's get in out of sight for a moment. We're being watched."

"We are. They will keep doing that until they trap us once more. And that is their plan."

"We know that. We need to take as many precautions as well can. But that may not be enough. What else do we need to plan?"

"I have no idea. I gather that we're living at your place. I'll need to make arrangements for this house."

"Take your time, love. It's no rush for that."

"I know. We'll pray through this just like we'll pray over any decision, big or small. Frank talked to me today. He said that Emma had sent information earlier in the week." Ashlynn reached for the salads that she had prepared, turning to find Torin setting the table for them.

"She was? That doesn't surprise me. What did he have to say?"

"That this goes back to the founding families in my town. And that somehow your family is involved. Have you talked to your dad at all?"

"Not really. He's been busy with the new charity he's been setting up. We can meet with them tomorrow and see what they have to say. I don't know that they would be aware of that."

"That's what I'm thinking." She sat, her hand in his as he said a blessing on their food. "The girls are all busy tomorrow but asked if we could meet on Sunday."

———

"We can. Here or at my place?"

"Here, I think. It will be the last time that we meet as a family in this home. They'll want that." Ashlynn grew sober, tears tickling at her eyes.

Torin gave a sound and then wrapped her into his arms.

"We'll get there, love. They can look on your new home as theirs."

"They will, but it won't be the same for them. This was their home for so many years. That is my new home and not theirs."

"I understand. And we'll make it theirs as much as we can."

Ashlynn nodded, her thoughts going back through the years, and the joys and sorrows that had flooded her home.

Chapter 26

Frank watched Ashlynn on the Monday morning as she paced his office. He had asked her to come in and she had agreed. Gerry had simply sent her on her way, telling her to come back when she could. He needed to speak with her about the investigation but she just wasn't cooperating with him.

"Ashlynn? Can you sit?" Frank watched as she did. "Are your plans ready for Saturday?"

"They are." Ashlynn bit at her lip. "Frank? Can I ask you something?"

"You know that you can."

"I need someone to walk me to Torin. You're the closest that I have to a brother. Would you do that?" She looked at him, blinking through tears.

"I would be honoured to, Ashlynn. That was one thing that I wanted to speak with you about." Frank looked down at the notes in the folder in front of him. "We'll talk more about that."

"But you need to talk to me about something else." Ashlynn drew a deep breath, somehow knowing that this would not be good.

"I do. This thing with your family? Rodney's been in touch. He's been working that exclusively now, he said. Did you know that your family was really rich at that time?"

Ashlynn shook her head.

"I don't know that any of us did. How does that come into what's going on now?"

"How does that come in? There is still a bank account and safety deposit box sitting there, waiting for the founder's family to come forward. We have proved that it's you and your girls. He hasn't said how much is there but that it is substantial. He said that your father was aware of it and was waiting until you had turned eighteen to speak with you and your brothers. Only he never got a chance. And the lawyer covered it so that you never knew. He has finally confessed to that and that he had planned to take over it all. There is not so much the money as the jewelry. Rodney needs a few more days to confirm everything but he wants to speak with you and the girls."

"Has this been what's it about? Our inheritance that we never knew about?"

"Not totally. That was the lawyer on his own. There is still whoever it is that is after you and Torin. And Torin does play into this somehow. Rodney is beginning to get a sense of why but had some information to confirm. He felt that might take a week or so."

"And we'll be away for ten days or so." Ashlynn drew in a deep breath. "Will this ever end, Frank? We're still be followed. I'm finding text messages that I keep sending on to you. So is Torin. There have been no more packages. And I have not had anyone in my house. But there is still someone out there."

———

"There is. I wish I could say that we would solve it this week. It's possible, God willing, that we could, but I don't get the sense that we will."

"No, you won't. We can keep everyone safe on Saturday?" Ashlynn was more worried than she wanted to admit.

"We have officers who have volunteered to be there. Some will be outside. Others will be inside posing as wedding guests. I know that you put it out that whoever wanted to come to the wedding could but only invite your friends and family to the tea. That isn't a problem. We'll keep you safe that day. And I understand that Ian has promised to fly you to your destination."

"He has. Abe found it for us. It's isolated but there is cell service. He's familiar with it and doesn't think anyone would find us. It's not associated in any way with us."

"Abe is good. He's done this for so many years he could do it in his sleep. And Richard will be there on Saturday. He promised me that he would."

"I did speak with him." Ashlynn stood. "If that's all, Frank, I need to get back to work. I want to get everything done in the next couple of days so that I can take the rest of the week off. Gerry is insisting on it."

"He is. And you will do what you can and the others will pick up for you. It's what you do for them. I don't know if you know how well loved you are in town, Ashlynn. You help without asking for anything in return. That is the same for Torin. You both work behind the scenes, helping your fellow townspeople. That is putting your faith to work. And it is being the light that you always taught your girls to be." Frank watched her walk away without saying anything.

Ashlynn stopped at Jeff's cafe to grab a meal, knowing that she wouldn't be back out for her lunch. Jeff watched her, knowing that she was troubled. He nodded as two youths that lived on the street followed her, watching carefully for anyone who was stalking her.

"They're watching out for her, aren't they, Lord? And thank you for that. Ashlynn would be missed greatly if anything were to happen to her."

Gerry watched Ashlynn closely that day. There was something different about her and he couldn't put a finger on what it was. It wasn't that she was getting married. That was not it.

"Ashlynn? What's up?" Gerry finally stood in her office doorway, his hands jammed into his pockets.

"Gerry? I'm not sure what you mean." Ashlynn stared at him, at a loss for what he meant.

"Something is up with you. What can I do to help?"

"With me?" Ashlynn drew in a deep breath. "I spoke with Frank this morning about my hometown. There are some issues there that I never knew about. Something that Dad had planned to talk to Aaron, Adam, and me and never had a chance to do so. I wish that he had. Maybe we wouldn't be in this situation if he had."

———

"Or you may still be. That's not something you could have known about."

"I know. It doesn't make it any easier, you know. And with Saturday coming up, I miss him."

"We know, Ashlynn. We wish that we could help that way but we can't. All we can do is pray for you. And that is what will get you through."

Ashlynn watched him walk away before her attention went back to her work. She was determined not to leave anything hanging over if she could help it. She looked up as she heard Torin's voice and then was on her feet, greeting him.

"You're here?" She leaned back in his arms to look at him.

"I am. Dad dropped me off. I plan on driving you home tonight, if I may?" He grinned at her as she nodded happily. "How soon will you be ready to go?"

"Now, I think." She quickly tidied up her desk, shut down her computer, and then reached for his hand, not seeing the looks and smiles being sent her way.

Chapter 27

The week passed quickly for Ashlynn. She didn't notice anyone watching her or following her but then there could have been. Her thoughts were elsewhere. Torin just watched her, content to know that she was safe for now. Her girls were at her home for as long as she would let them during the day, finally leaving when she sent them home.

Heather approached Ashlynn on the Friday afternoon, hugging her and then standing with her hands on the younger lady's arms.

"What can I do for you, Ashlynn? Is there anything that needs to be done?"

Ashlynn looked around, a frown on her face.

"No, I think we have everything organized. Other than my packing to move to Torin's. I haven't done that as yet and I need to."

"Okay, so that's what we do. Sue is on her way and I hear tell Meg is too. Let us help you do that. Where do you want to start?"

"My office, I guess. I need to pack up the computer and what I need to take from there." Ashlynn headed that way, stopping for a moment to see that the office had already been packed up and moved. "When did this happen?"

"Your office? I think Torin and Tyrel did it not that long ago. You didn't know?"

"No, I didn't." Ashlynn reached for her phone to send off a quick text. She drew a breath of relief to hear that he was setting up her computer in his office. "He has it. I thought for a moment it had been stolen."

"And that is a fear you are living with, isn't it? Okay, so now what? Your kitchen?"

"We did that last night, taking over anything that was perishable. We'll clear it out when we're back. We need to sort through everything." Ashlynn grew pensive. "I'm just so torn as to what to keep and what not to keep."

"You're not giving up your house right away, are you? Then leave what you need for now. What are your plans for the house?"

"I plan to sell it, I think." Ashlynn headed for her bedroom, stopping for a moment, seeing the bags that were packed. "Who did this?"

"Your nieces were around this morning. I think that they did this." Heather grinned at her. "So, now what? Everything that you were wanting to pack is now done. So what can I do for you?"

Ashlynn shrugged.

"I'm not sure, Heather. I want this over and now but it won't be. I still don't understand the why's of it."

"We understand that, Ashlynn. Here, sit for a moment. Let me pray for you and Torin. This is a huge step to take at any time but going through this makes it even harder. We'll pray and then we'll talk it through. Tell me about your childhood and anything that you can remember from then."

Ashlynn stared at her, blinking rapidly for a moment.

"No one has asked me to do that, you know. That's what I need to do." Ashlynn's head bowed as Heather began to pray.

Neither lady heard the door open and close and then soft footsteps heading their way. Torin and Troye just sat near their ladies, ready to take up the prayer as the ladies finished.

Ashlynn sat with her head down for a few moments, just resting in the prayers that had been raised. She felt Torin's arm around her and she leaned against him.

"Torin, your mom asked me to talk about my childhood. No one has asked me to do that."

"No? Then that's what we do. We'll work on it for a while. Then we sat to take you ladies out for a meal if we can. We've reserved a room at the local Italian restaurant. Your girls will meet us there." He reached to kiss her, sitting back to watch her.

"Okay. So, where do I start?"

"Just start talking, Ashlynn. I'll do a recording of it, if you wish. That way we can go back over what you've said." Troye held up his phone.

"That's a wonderful idea, Troye. Thank you." Ashlynn thought back to her childhood, a wishful look crossing her face. "I really miss my Mom and Dad. I want them here and they're not."

"We know that, sweetheart. We want them here for you as well. But they're not. So, what can you tell me?" Torin's arms tightened around her.

"I really don't know what to say. This is hard, you know." Ashlynn's eyes slid closed for a moment as her thoughts shifted back in time.

Ashlynn's first memories were with her brothers, who were a number of years older than her. She was loved by them and loved them just as much back in return. She was determined to do things for herself, standing up to them with a frown on her face as they simply grinned at her.

Her parents adored her but didn't spoil her. That was not who they were. Her father didn't talk about his work and Ashlynn was not sure even to that day exactly what his work was. She knew that it was legal. There were not many extended family members who were in her life. Ashlynn had asked about that once and had simply been told that her parents didn't have a lot to do with their families. And that had satisfied her at the time. Only it no longer did.

"Mom and Dad didn't have a lot to do with their families. I never knew why. I don't have any information on them." Ashlynn blinked as she looked over at Troye. "Is there a way that we can look into them?"

"There is, Ashlynn. Ronan said that a friend of his has a family tree program that she has been working through for you. She has information for you and has passed on what she can to Frank. She'll be in touch once you two are back."

Ashlynn nodded, her thoughts troubled.

"Have we heard anything more about the lawyer?" Ashlynn was desperate to hear that everyone had been found and she could move forward with her life without being afraid.

"He's not involved in this, Ashlynn. That much has been determined. We just don't have enough information at this point to tell you who is behind this. It has not been forgotten." Troye watched with compassion as Ashlynn fought to control her emotions.

Chapter 28

The next afternoon, Torin turned from facing the front of the church, his eyes moving past the young ladies to find his love. Ashlynn stood at the door into the sanctuary, her hand tucked into Frank's arm. Frank had offered to take the place of one of her brothers to walk her to Torin, and she had gladly accepted. He had become like a brother to her over the years, stepping into that role over the years for her.

"You're a beautiful lady, Ashlynn. And you are loved by that man waiting for you." Frank had prayed for her before they had approached the door.

"Thank you, Frank. You have been there for me so much over the years, particularly in the last year or so." Ashlynn reached to kiss his cheek. "Now, let's get this show on the road." She laughed as he grinned at her.

Ashlynn simply tucked her hand into Torin's as they moved through the ceremony. Afterwards, neither one of them could remember exactly what happened. They watched their friends and families mingle with one another.

"Happy, sweetheart?" Torin's arms were around his bride, his eyes on her.

"I am, Torin. And you?" She felt his nod against the top of her head. "I'm just so afraid." She moved away at that point, towards her nieces who had turned towards her.

The four younger men stood shoulder to shoulder with Torin, just supporting him.

"Torin? What can we do for you over the next week? Do we need to watch your home for you?" Gareth spoke up at last.

"No, it's good. You're watching Ashlynn's home. That's enough. Frank has arranged for an officer to check the outsides of both over the next week. Dad or Tyrel will go through mine."

That evening, Ashlynn turned from the church, her eyes on Torin as he drove away. They were away for the next week, she knew, a time that was desperately needed. A friend had made arrangements for them to fly out to an isolated island and then back in six days.

A week later, Torin walked through his home, nodding to himself. His mother had been through, he could tell, fresh flowers in the rooms. He knew that would have been from Eilis' shop. He could hear Ashlynn singing softly to herself as she worked in the kitchen. They had felt safe and protected over the last week. Now that they were home, he felt fear once more. He had reached out to Frank, only able to leave a voice mail for him, simply stating that they were home and what was the update.

Torin stared down at his desk and the pile of mail. He reached to sort through it, setting aside six envelopes. He frowned, staring down at his and Ashlynn's names. He would need to open them with her. But right now, he just wanted their homecoming to be peaceful and happy. He turned as he felt a hand on his back and wrapped Ashlynn in his arms.

"What are those?" Ashlynn pointed to the envelopes.

"Mail that we need to open, sweetheart. Only I don't want to." Torin simply stood, content to hold the love of his life in his arms.

Ashlynn moved away from him at last, reaching for the letter opener and then slitting open the envelopes. She placed each one in the order that it seemed to have been received in. Torin reached for the first one, a prayer uttered before he pulled out the piece of paper. Ashlynn followed his movements, opening each envelope and stapling the envelope to the letter. Her hand reached for Torin's as she looked up at him.

"Torin? What are these?" Ashlynn was puzzled as she read each letter. "They don't make sense. Or do they?"

Torin paused, his mind racing for a moment. He reached for his camera, taking photos of each letter, before he was uploading them to his computer.

"I'll send them on to Emma. She'll look at them. And we need to get them to Frank or Adam." He watched Ashlynn as she paced the office. "Ashlynn? What are your thoughts?"

"That this is not what it seems. These are not threatening, are they? It's almost as if they are in a cryptic code or something. Is it someone trying to help us instead of threatening us?'

Torin's hand paused on the keyboard, his eyes thoughtful.

"Just what are you saying, sweetheart?"

Ashlynn shoved over the letters so that she could perch on the desk. She rubbed at her face before she clasped her hands together, her eyes on the waterfall picture across the room from her. She appreciated the pictures of nature that Torin had filled his house with. They were ones that she would have chosen.

"You think someone is trying to tell you something?" Torin's mind was racing before he nodded. "That makes sense, you know. Someone is trying to help you get to the bottom of whatever it is that happened all those years ago." Torin spun his chair, staring at the door before he was back around, his hands reaching for hers. "So, what are your thoughts?"

"I'm not sure. I have no idea who would do this. It has to be someone from my past. Maybe someone who knew either Aaron or Adam."

"Okay, so we start listing who their friends are. At least, these are not threatening." Ashlynn reached for the first one, a frown on her face. "Can we call in our families these or should we work on them ourselves?"

"By ourselves for now. I know Ronan's friends would help." Torin sighed. "Let me call Tyrel. He works as an insurance investigator. He loves cryptic puzzles. He may have a thought."

"Send them to him by email. We are not approaching any of our families today. We're not supposed to be back until tonight, remember?" She smirked at him as he reached to kiss her.

"You are so right. That cabin in the woods was wonderful. Ian said that Abe's uncle owns it and not too many people know about it. He also said that they used it for one of his teammates and his girlfriend at one time."

"I can see that. We need to find a retreat like that. Only I would prefer that it have a road into it." She sighed as she rose. "It's lunchtime, Torin. I have food ready for us. Only I'm not sure that I feel like eating."

Torin was on his feet, an arm around her, as he turned them towards the hallway.

"Let's eat and then we pray. We need to bathe ourselves in prayer for the next while. I fear for our safety."

"Me too. I just wish this was over. We can't really move on when we are afraid for one another."

"No, we can't." Torin set the plates on the table and reached to pour their coffee. He sat, his hand reaching for hers as he asked the blessing on their food, adding a fervent prayer for their safety and a swift resolution to their adventure.

Chapter 29

Brinn walked towards her aunt the next morning, a frown on her face. Something had happened, she decided, and turned to Gareth.

"Gareth? Something has happened with Aunt Ash."

Gareth nodded, having come to the same conclusion.

"I agree. Are we meeting for lunch today?"

"We are. At Aunt Ash's." Brian sighed to herself. "This is hard, you know. I have to change how I view Torin's place now that it's Aunt Ash's."

"It is hard to do that but it will come." Gareth shut the car door behind Brinn, having seen Ashlynn and Torin drive away.

"It will." Brinn watched carefully around them, not seeing anyone who stood out.

Ashlynn greeted her nieces and their husbands and then stood watching them. She sighed. This was not going well, she decided.

Torin moved among the younger people, his eyes watchful. He lifted his eyes to study his bride and nodded. She had peace at last, he decided, their prayers at work. He turned as he heard Flynn speaking with him.

"What was that, Flynn"

"What's going on, Torin? Something has changed." Flynn studied his uncle now by marriage.

"There has been a change. We received letters in the mail that we opened yesterday. Not threatening." Torin frowned for a moment. "Ashlynn and I think that someone is trying to help us."

Ronan shared a look with Declan, who nodded.

"That's what we wondered about what the ladies received. There was no threat with them. It has been a puzzle why they have been getting the parcels." Declan turned for a moment, searching for Eilis.

"There has been no threat. And the investigator from their hometown has not been able to explain that. The lawyer denies knowing anything about it." Torin watched the two younger men.

"That's what Chani has said." Ronan shook his head. None of them had ever been able to explain the parcels. "Tag has been working on it for us as has Evan. Neither of them had been able to determine exactly what is going on with that."

"Maybe there will be a clue in the letters. Where are they?" Declan turned towards the office as Torin pointed that way.

The younger men took the copies of the letters that they were handed and then found seats. Silence was in the room as they read through them, with just the soft rustling of paper as they shifted from one to another. Flynn looked up at one point, frowning before he was on his feet, heading for the map that Torin had hanging on his wall.

Torin followed him, waiting for Flynn to speak.

"Flynn? What have you discovered?"

Flynn shrugged, not quite sure what he had discovered.

"It was just a thought, Torin. We know that their family goes way back in their town. Who else goes back that far? Have we ever discovered that? Or is it someone from a neighbouring town who wanted to move in and couldn't? And now a family member is trying to help Ashlynn and the ladies out."

"That's what we're thinking, Flynn. Ashlynn asked about that this morning. We have reached out to the investigator before church, just asking that question." Torin reached to hug Ashlynn to him. She had approached them, a puzzled look on her face.

"Torin? Flynn? What are you thinking?"

"That someone is trying to help you, just like we talked about." Torin watched her face, seeing as she had a thought. "What did you think about just now?"

"That maybe we need to go back there again. Jeff may have some ideas for us."

"We can email him, Ashlynn, without going back there. He's been emailing me since we were there." Torin turned as he heard the other young men approaching. "You've discovered something?"

"We think so, Torin." Gareth stared down at his papers. "There is a clue in here. Very basic but I think that we need to find someone who can go over what we've found."

"Try Abe and his men." Ashlynn turned to him. "They will do that for us. In fact, I wouldn't be surprised to see some of them appear this week." Ashlynn walked away, determined that she would not break down in front of her family.

Tori sighed and then excused himself to walk after her. He found her on the back porch, an arm wrapped around a column. He simply swept her into his arms, a prayer whispering in her ear.

"Ashlynn, sweetheart, what are you thinking?"

"I'm thinking that maybe Dad knew something about this. I have his paperwork. It's locked in a safety deposit box. I went through it a couple of years ago but not from this point of view. We need to retrieve it and do that."

"We can. I have meeting all day tomorrow and you need to work." Torin was unsure how to proceed and that disturbed him. "Maybe over the lunch hour?"

"We can do that. We need to go back in with the girls and their fellows." Ashlynn turned in his arms, hugging him, She felt safe and secure with him.

"We do, but I like it out here with you." Torin grinned at her before he kissed her. He turned them back towards the door, a frown on his face for a moment.

"So do I." Ashlynn moved away from him once they were back in the house. A thought had crossed her mind and she needed to search the paperwork that had been brought over from her home. Maybe, just maybe, there was something in there that would help today.

Chapter 30

Ashlynn's hands rested on the safety deposit box, uncertainty in her stance. Torin stood close beside her, an arm around her. He knew that she was unsettled in what she might find. They had prayed many times over this very action through the past few hours.

"Ashlynn? I can open it for you." Torin's voice was soft and full of worry for her.

"No, it's okay." She unlocked it and lifted the top, her hands pausing before she reached to remove the papers. She stared down into the empty box, her thoughts mixed. She knew that once she started going through them again, there would be no going back. She just prayed that there would be an answer in them.

Torin gently removed the papers from Ashlynn's hand and dropped them into his briefcase, locking it after he close it. He searched her face before wrapping her into his arms. She shuddered for a moment before she simply hugged him back, reaching to kiss him.

"Thank you, Torin. You are my rock in all this."

That evening, Torin reached for his briefcase, unlocking it and removing the paperwork. He paused, his head turning as he heard Ashlynn's voice. She was on the phone with Frank, simply stating that they had cleared out her safety deposit box and promising him that if they found anything, they would be in touch.

Ashlynn paused for a moment in the doorway until she almost ran toward Torin and his open arms.

She sobbed for a moment, sorrow filling her heart and thoughts as she remembered her parents and her brothers and their wives. This just seemed such a final act at this point, one that there was no stopping or going back from.

Torin simply held his bride, waiting for her to move. She had to make that first move. He could not and would not do that for her. He was patient in his waiting, his thoughts turning to prayer and petition for protection and answers. Torin knew that this was not over, not by a long shot as the saying went.

"Ashlynn? We don't have to do this tonight. We can wait." Torin had booked the next day off from his duties and had spoken with Gerry and done the same for Ashlynn. She had just looked at him and nodded, thanking him quietly for his thoughtfulness and care. She had not had that for many years, she thought, far too many years.

Ashlynn reached for the first paper, unfolding it and reading it, handing it to Torin. Torin read it, noting that it was just a receipt for the mortgage on the house being paid off.

"Your house, Ashlynn? What happened to it?"

"The house? We sold it when I turned eighteen and split the profits. That's how I was able to afford my home here." She blinked rapidly, her thoughts on her parents. "Mom and Dad made sure that we were taken care of. They had worked hard to pay off their home." She tapped the receipt. "That's the proof."

"It is indeed." Torin reached for the next paper and then the next. He had finally reached for file folders, neatly labeling them and then stacking them on his desk. His eyes were on Ashlynn as she reached for the last envelope.

"I never opened this. I just didn't have the heart." Ashlynn's tears flowed down her face. "This is Dad's handwriting. Maybe if I had read it, Aaron and Adam would still be alive."

"Not likely, Ashlynn. Their deaths are not related to this. I spoke with the investigator from your hometown earlier. He wants to meet with us tomorrow. He had finally solved that accident that they had."

"He has? Okay, but I have to work. No, I don't. You booked us off. Is this why?" She looked up at him, a lost little girl look on her face that caused him to simply wrap her into a hug.

"It is. That and what we're doing now. I didn't think either one of us would be ready to face anyone tomorrow. God had told me that."

"And you listen to what He tells you. That is such a blessing to have that in my life, someone who listens and obeys God."

"And you do as well, sweetheart." Torin turned her to the couch in his office, seating her and then disappearing. He returned a few moments later, a tray with mugs of coffee on it for them. "Here. Let's spend some time in prayer about this. If we don't sleep tonight, then we don't. But this is something that is weighing heavily on you. I can see that. Once we've read it, it will change what you have believed all your life, I suspect."

"I'm sure that it will. It scares me, Torin, and I don't scare easily. I worry for my girls."

"I know that you don't. And I know that you are. It's only human to worry about those we love, even though God is in control."

Ashlynn nodded, turning as Torin drew her close to him, an arm wrapped around her. She heard his prayer and the promises that he quoted in his prayer. She relaxed against him, thankful that he was in her life, that he was her light in life to follow.

Ashlynn's eyes opened and she stared at the envelope before she sighed. This would not open on its own, she knew, and reached for the letter opened that Torin handed her. She had ignored her phone that evening, knowing that her girls were trying to reach her. She just couldn't speak with them until she had read this letter. And even then she wasn't sure that she could.

Torin's arm tightened around her. He knew that this may well change what she thought about her family. He prayed that it didn't. She didn't need to have her memories destroyed. Torin was afraid that just would be what happened. Abe had been in touch with them, letting them know that his team was working on the letters and had managed to crack the first one. That was leading to the others being cracked. He hoped to have a report for him by the next day.

Ashlynn removed the papers from the envelope, a frown on her face at the number.

"This is strange, Torin. What was Dad doing?" She looked up at him and then back at the papers.

———

"I have no idea. Let's look through them, read them, and then make a decision on what we need to do. At some point, we'll need to meet with your girls, I suspect."

"I know we will." Ashlynn still stared across the room, not seeing the comfortable furnishings, the photos and paintings on the walls, the built-in bookcases that were well filled. She puzzled in her mind what her father may have been up to and just couldn't figure it out.

Torin simply waited, content to hold her, and knowing that she would read the papers when she could. He had spoken with Frank that afternoon. There was no news on whoever it was that was after Ashlynn. That was a puzzle to them both. Whoever it was seemed to have gone quiet. Torin worried even more at that. If they were not open with trying to terrorize her, then they had no way of knowing where they were or even who they were.

Chapter 31

Ashlynn began to read the letter, tears briefly clouding her eyes at she saw her father's handwriting. She was puzzled at the words and looked up at Torin.

"Torin? I don't understand what Dad is saying."

Torin dropped a kiss on her forehead, puzzled as well.

"Let's read it and then go from there. He may have answers that we need."

Ashlynn nodded, her eyes back on the letter.

"Dear Aaron, Adam, and Ashlynn

"If you are reading this, then the talk that your mother and I planned to have with you when Ashlynn turned eighteen has not happened. That thought saddens me.

"Aaron and Adam? You have become the men of God that you were raised to be. We are so proud of both of you and the families that you are raising. You have not disappointed us in any way.

"Ashlynn, our beloved daughter. You are a joy to be around, a source of inspiration and encouragement. We pray that whatever you have attempted in your life has been successful.

"You three children have been the delight and love of our lives. We have often spoken of just that. If we have at any time neglected to tell you, rest assured

———

that our intention was not to ignore that. We can only pray that we have shown it by our actions.

"Now, the house. It is yours to use whichever one of you want to do that. If none of you do, then sell it and divide the proceeds. We put no restrictions on how you may use it. That decision is yours alone, yours and God's.

"Now, as to what has happened in the past. You three know that we have not had contact with any of our relatives. We have none. Your grandparents died when you were young, Aaron and Adam. Ashlynn never met them. My sister died from cancer when she was a teen. Your mother's sister and brother both died young, her from heart disease, him from a heart attack. It has always been our regret that you could not know them. There were no families on either side to be left behind.

"If you research our family, you will find our roots go back to the beginning of the town, many years ago. We were not one of the original founding families but we did arrive about ten years later. Our family has always been involved in the law and order portion of it, until myself. I chose to take another route in life, that of a printer. I was involved in counselling for trouble youth. They have always been a burden on me. Your mother just wanted to stay home and raise you three. That was okay with me.

"Now, there is a dear friend who has moved to another town. If in the future, you need to know anything about our history or families that you can't find, speak with him. Stephen Steele is his name. He grew up in the house next door to us and was a friend *for life. He has never met your children, by his choice as he moved away before any of you were born. But he knows you and has prayed for you daily. Talk to him.*

"If I could say anything else, it would be to stay true to your faith. Keep your lamps burning at all times, to be ready to answer for your faith. More importantly, watch for God in your daily walk, for the moments when He appears and speaks with you.

"You have our love, you three. Aaron, our first-born, Adam, our second son, and Ashlynn, the little girl who we dreamed about and never thought would ever grace our home. We cannot tell you how much you have enriched our lives. That we don't have the words for.

"All our love.

"Mom and Dad."

Ashlynn carefully folded the letter and placed it back into the envelope. Torin reached for it, setting it on the table beside her, before he tightened his arms around her. Ashlynn did not weep. She could not. She was numb from what the letter had said. She had known that she was loved but to hear it from beyond the grave was something that she had to deal with. Right now, that wasn't possible.

"We need to show the girls, Torin." Ashlynn sighed, her eyes closing at the thought.

"We will. We'll get copies for them. It is a treasured letter from your parents. I don't think that if you had read it before, it would have meant as much to you as it does now."

"Has he been the one, Torin?"

"The one? Who, sweetheart?"

"The one sending us those parcels. He would have known that the boys were dead. He could have come around and no one would have thought anything about it. There were still family members in town." She looked up at him. "If it has been, why?"

"That's what we'll ask him. We'll reach out to him, Ashlynn. Tomorrow, we'll call him. I'll have someone look him up first."

Ashlynn was on her feet, sorting through the papers on his desk, and then back beside him.

"Here. Emma sent this. I set it aside as I didn't recognize him. She's found information on him." Ashlynn handed him the paper. "We'll need to speak with her, I think."

Torin nodded, his phone vibrating disturbing him. He had been ignoring it and finally just couldn't.

"Abe's just sent a message. They want to head this way tomorrow." Torin sent a quick message and nodded at Abe's response. "They'll come by in the morning."

"That's good." Ashlynn grew quiet, fatigue suddenly setting in. Her emotions were in a turmoil and she felt that she could not even pray at this point. She knew that was when the Holy Spirit would pray for her. She had that confidence

Torin was content just to sit, hold his bride, and pray for her and for himself. Perhaps they would have more answers on the morrow but he could not even comprehend what the answers would be. Neither of them could.

Frank turned as he heard his name called. Ian and Nathaniel were walking towards him. He frowned that two of Abe's security team were there.

"Frank? Do you have time for a meal?" Ian pointed towards the diner.

"I do. But I don't think that you're here just for a meal."

"We are, but we do have information to pass on to you. Abe didn't want to wait." Ian slid onto the bench seat and moved over so that Nathaniel could sit beside him. "There are some things that have come up that he didn't feel could wait for a courier or email."

"I see." Frank nodded at the waitress, knowing that a meal would soon appear in front of them.

"And you're here because of Ashlynn?"

"We are. There are circumstances that have arisen. Information that was not available in the past that has now come to light."

Frank nodded, having come to that conclusion himself.

Chapter 32

Abe watched Ashlynn closely the next morning, knowing that Emma had information to share with her. Somehow, he seemed to know that Ashlynn was aware of some of what they had to say.

Emma turned to Ashlynn, assessing her and then reaching for her hands. She prayed for her friend before she reached for the folder which she had set to one side.

"Emma? What do you have to tell me?" Ashlynn felt Torin's arm around her.

"I have news, Ashlynn, and I just don't know how to tell you this." Emma drew in a deep breath. "We have tracked down a friend of your father's. Stephen Steele."

"He's the one who was mentioned in Dad's letter. Have you spoken with him?"

"I have. By the phone yesterday. He was not aware that you didn't know him. He thought that you would have heard about him."

"Dad never mentioned him, not that I remember. And I think that I would have. And I don't remember Aaron or Adam talking about him." Ashlynn's brow furrowed as she tried to remember if she had heard of the Steele family.

"That's what Stephen has said. He is the one who has sent the girls and you the items. He was able to retrieve them before the lawyer removed the jewelry boxes. He tracked him down and forced him to return them. However, he was never sure if the lawyer had returned everything. He thought that by sending you what he had, you would come back to your town and speak with the neighbours and that way he could get in touch with you. Only you never did that. You never spoke with the neighbours.”

“No, we didn’t. We drove by the house but didn’t stop. I’m not sure that any of the neighbours would have mentioned him.”

“They may not have. The houses have changed hands over the years.” Abe shared a look with Torin who nodded. “Now, he does want to speak with you. He’ll come here to your town. For some reason he is afraid for you to come back there.”

“I don’t understand that. The investigator has said that he has solved the murders of my brothers. He’s heading here this weekend to speak with the girls and me. I’m not sure that I am ready to hear that.”

Emma’s hands tightened on Ashlynn’s. She bit at her lips for a moment.

“Ashlynn, you have met Darci. Have her come here then and meet with you all and Stephen. She has offered to do that. She and Doug are available on Saturday.”

“That would work. Have Stephen call me and set up a time.” Torin drew in a deep breath. “Things have changed for us with this letter and now the investigation being over for Ashlynn’s brothers. That will bring closure for that for the girls and Ashlynn. Now, can we set this aside? We’ll need to reach out to

Frank unless you have already. Ashlynn needs to do something fun. What can we get up to?"

Abe began to laugh even as Emma smirked at the other couple.

"Come with us. Our guys and their ladies are here. Their children are being looked after for the day so that they could come here."

Ashlynn's face lit up at that.

"Oh, that's wonderful. What are we up to?"

Torin simply smiled, happy that his bride was happy.

Frank stood at their front door late that afternoon. It had been a very busy day. He had hoped to be there earlier but that had not worked out. He stepped back a couple of steps just to watch the area and nodded. Someone had put in more cameras for Torin and he was glad to see that.

Torin watched Frank for a moment from where he stood in the open front doorway. Frank was troubled, he could see, and burning out.

"Frank?" Torin's voice startled the other man who spun at his voice.

"Torin? I didn't hear the door open." Frank moved into the house, seeing Ashlynn waiting for him. "Ashlynn? You're okay?"

"I think so, Frank, but I'm not really sure any more. You have news? But first, we have coffee and sweets. Then, we'll talk. I still have to return Sue's call."

"No rush on that, Ashlynn. She just wanted to see what day you two could do lunch."

Frank sat back at last, his eyes closing for a moment. He was exhausted and due off duty for the next couple for the next couple of days. He needed that desperately.

"Ashlynn? You said something about a letter from your father?"

Ashlynn nodded, on her feet to retrieve the copy that she had made for him.

"Here." She handed it to him before sitting again. "Emma has researched the man named and reached out to him. We're to meet on Saturday with the girls."

Frank studied her, his keen eyes not missing much, before his gaze turned to Torin. He nodded. Things were coming to a head, he thought, and not how they had expected. He read through the letter, pausing at the man's name. He knew him, he realized, and that was in a good way. He was glad. Ashlynn and her girls didn't need any more danger than they were in or had been in.

"Emma did send me information on him, but I have not been in the office to read through it all. You're content with what she has told you?" Frank watched Ashlynn closely.

"I am, Frank. I am. Dad's talked about him in the letter and Dad would not have mentioned him if there had been any concern. I wish Dad had spoken earlier about him but I understand why."

———

Torin walked away for a moment, a troubled thought crossing his mind. He sent a quick text off to Emma, who responded quickly. She had had the same thought and was working through it. Evan would be in touch in the next day or so with what they had found. She was unable to come back but he was willing to. And she thought that his friends would be there as well.

Ashlynn walked through the house late that night. She knew that Torin was on a call that he had not wanted to take but had had no choice on. She sat on the couch, comfortable enough to know that he would not object. He had smiled at her, his face lighting up as she appeared.

Torin set his phone down and rose, coming to sit beside Ashlynn.

"You're okay, sweetheart?"

"I am, love. Emma called earlier."

"She did? I wondered if she would. Did she say anything?"

"As in that you called her when Frank was here and that she had had the same thought that you had? Now, I understand Evan and his friends will head this way."

"They will. Let's set this aside for the night, sweetheart. We need to start spending time in prayer and Bible study together. This is a good time of night to do so."

"It is. I'm glad you suggested that. I wanted to but wasn't sure if you would."

"Never be afraid to talk to me about things like this, Ashlynn. We're partners in life. Something like this will draw us closer together."

Chapter 33

On the Thursday evening, the four young ladies stared at their aunt and then at one another. They were not sure what she had just said. Ashlynn simply stood, her hands gripping the back of a chair in the kitchen, an unreadable look on her face.

"Aunt Ash? What are you saying?" Brinn finally spoke, her voice sounding loud in the kitchen.

"That I read a letter that Dad wrote. Finally. I have had it for years in the safety deposit box. I just didn't realize that it was so important. I'm sorry." Ashlynn tamped down her emotions, not wanting to break down in front of the girls.

"I heard that but what did it say?" It was Chani's turn to speak. Her arm was around Eilis, both young ladies not sure what their aunt had meant.

"I have copies for you." Ashlynn turned to the counter, hesitated for a moment, and then reached for the papers that she and Torin had prepared. They had spent time praying over it all, just to find the peace that they needed. Only, it wasn't so easy to find. "Here. These are copies of the letter. It was addressed to your fathers and myself."

The young ladies took the papers, glancing at one another before they found seats. There was quiet in the kitchen for a few moments, quiet that was except for the rustle of turning papers.

Darbi looked up at last, her eyes on her aunt.

"Aunt Ash? Who is this man that Grandpa spoke about?"

"The man? I have no idea who he is. We are to meet with him this Saturday. Frank and Adam will be here. I want to hear what he has to say." Ashlynn slid into a seat, suddenly exhausted. She was ready to have this over with. She and Torin had plans for their lives and this was preventing them from happening.

"We'll be here. What can we do in the meantime?" Eilis rose to hug her aunt, her eyes on the clock. "I'm sorry. I have to run. We have a meeting to be at tonight." Eilis was gone before anyone could say anything.

Torin walked through the house later that evening, searching for Ashlynn. He found her curled up in the sunroom, a blanket wrapped around her. He stood watching her for a few moments before he walked over, scooped her into his arms, and sat back into her place on the love seat.

"Okay, sweetheart?" His voice was barely above a whisper.

Ashlynn shrugged, not sure if she was.

"The girls were here earlier. They have questions that we don't have the answers for. And I feel as if I am to blame for not reading that letter earlier."

"God knows why you didn't. It wasn't time for you to find it and read it. Now it is. God's timing is perfect."

They sat in quiet for a while before Ashlynn sighed and rose. She headed for the kitchen, to tidy it for the night. She stood, staring down at the sink, not sure where they were heading but she could feel the storm and its danger approaching.

Saturday morning, Frank and Adam approached the house, frowning at the couple standing on the steps. Frank's brown clear.

"Doug? Darci? You're here?" Frank reached to greet them.

"We are. Do you know if Ashlynn and Torin are home? We've been here for about ten minutes without any answer to our knocks." Darci turned to stare at the house door. "I'm not getting a very good feeling."

Frank was away around the house, Adam towards the garage. Doug shared a look with Darci and then followed Frank. He paused as he entered the backyard, sensing something was off. A sudden yell from Frank had him spinning and then running his way, calling for Darci to call 911.

Frank was on his knees, hands reaching to turn Torin to his back. His face hardened as he saw the congealing blood on his chest. A hand reached for the wrist, checking for a pulse.

Doug was beside him, assessing Torin as well. He lifted his head as Darci's hand rested on his shoulder.

"Is he alive, Doug?" Darci was almost afraid to ask.

"He is, Darci." Frank turned as Adam approached. "Adam?"

"No sign of Ashlynn, Frank. I've been through the house. We'll need to bring in a team." Adam was frustrated. This wasn't supposed to happen. Ashlynn was not to have disappeared. Torin was not to be in a life-threatening condition.

Frank watched as the paramedics worked on Torin. He was afraid for his friend, not knowing how long it had been. Adam stood beside him and then moved away with the paramedics as they wheeled the stretcher towards the street. He was intending on riding with Torin.

Doug turned from studying the yard, his eyes on Darci, who shook her head. This is not how they had planned to meet with the other couple.

"Frank? Any word on what happened?" Doug stopped beside him, a hand reaching for Darci's.

"No, none. Ashlynn has gone missing. Torin is hurt. And we have no idea who. And that man from her hometown is to be here." Frank walked away, Doug and Darci following him. He headed for the man standing by a car, his arms crossed across his chest.

"Are you Stephen Steele?" Frank's identification was out. "You were to meet with Torin and Ashlynn this morning?"

"I am. What's going on? They didn't call me to cancel." Stephen's face showed his confusion and concern.

"For starters, Torin is on his way to the hospital. He is injured. Ashlynn is missing. Would you know anything about that?" Frank's voice was hard. His friends were hurt or missing and he wanted to find Ashlynn without anything else happening to her.

"Nothing." Stephen stared down at the ground before he handed over a thick manilla envelope. "This may explain what is happening to her. I guess that I need to speak with you."

"You do. We'll head to our detachment and meet there." He watched as an officer approached Stephen and then walked off with him. "Doug, you and Darci are staying around?"

"We are. We've made arrangements to say over until Monday. Where can we help?" Doug turned as he heard a female voice calling Frank's name.

"With the girls and their guys. You can work with them." He eyed the envelope in his hands. "Let me make a copy of it and get it to you. The girls need to know what is in this."

Chapter 34

Troye and Heather rose as the surgeon walked their way. They had planned on being away that afternoon. Frank's phone call had changed their plans.

"Brad? What is the word?" Troye greeted the surgeon, a friend from church.

"He's a fortunate man, Troye, Heather. God had His hand on him. He should be dead and he's not." He watched as Troye's arm came around Heather to keep her on her feet. Tyrel stood on the other side of his mother.

"Why do you say that?" Troye kept his eyes on Brad.

"He's alive, Troye. He should be dead. As you are aware, he was shot in the chest. It was from a distance, I understand, and that helped to slow down the force of the bullet. That helped to mitigate any damage. That being said, he did a lot of bleeding. He was there on the ground for a while. We're not sure for how long. Not moving helped to stop the bleeding. Now, as to what we need to do now? We're prepping him for surgery. We'll need your consent to do so as Ashlynn isn't here. Where is she?" He looked at the three as they simply stood silent.

"We don't know, Brad. We really don't. She wasn't in the house when they found Torin."

Five hours later, Troye walked away from his son's hospital room. His emotions were in a turmoil. He looked around for someone who could give him any information on the investigation but no one was there. He frowned at the couple who stood watching him.

Doug walked towards Troye, his eyes thoughtful.

"Mr. Callahan? I'm Doug Foster and this is my wife, Darci. I'm a police officer in Riverville and my wife is a retired forensics psychologist. We were to meet with Torin and Ashlynn this morning at Emma and Abe's request."

"You were? What about?"

Doug pointed to the chairs and waited as Troye sank down, his fatigue evident.

"What can we do for you, Mr. Callahan?" Darci's hand rested on his even as she prayed for him.

"For me? I have no idea. And please, call me Troye." Troye rested his head back against the wall. He prayed for his son and then for his daughter-in-law.

"Yes, for you." Doug simply prayed for his friend's father.

Frank approached at that point. He sat down near the trio, his eyes watchful. He had no further information on what happened to Torin. And he had no idea where Ashlynn was. Frank turned as he heard footsteps and then was on his feet, wrapping Brinn into a hug. She sobbed against him, Gareth standing nearby, unable to help his wife. The other three couples were there as well, uncertain as to what they were to do or where they needed to be.

"Frank? How's Torin?" Flynn asked the question that they were all avoiding.

"He's in a room now. He came through surgery fine. His mother and brother are with him." Frank nodded towards the chairs.

The group sat, quiet among them. They were worried about their aunt, Frank knew, and he had no information to help them. He needed to work through what Stephen had provided and had a detective working on that for him. At the moment, he was searching for Ashlynn. Only he had no way of knowing exactly where she was.

A week passed. Torin was at home, lost and hurting. He hurt as his body tried to heal but his heart hurt even more, not having his beloved Ashlynn there. Frank and Adam had been around, trying to help but not able to offer any information on where Ashlynn was or why she had been taken.

Torin turned that day from his desk. He was working as best he could from home but really needed to head for his office the next day. He had no heart for that. Reaching for the envelope that Frank had dropped on his desk that day, Torin prayed, sensing that this would change everything. When asked, Frank had simply said that it was what Stephen Steele had provided him. And that Torin needed to go over it by himself and with the girls.

He heard the door open and close and then footsteps heading his way. Tyrel appeared, a tray with coffees on it in his head.

"Torin? Should you be up?" Tyrel didn't push his brother, simply handed him the cup of coffee.

"No, I shouldn't be, but I need to be. Does that even make sense?" Torin sighed. "This is hard, Ty. I want Ashlynn here but I don't know if she'll be alive or dead when she comes back."

"No, we don't know that. That's in God's hands. And it is a difficult decision to come to, to be willing to let God have His way."

"It is, Ty. We've talked about this so many times. Say, how is Lily?" Torin grinned as his brother just smiled.

"She's fine. Worried about you two. We're moving ahead with our wedding plans but won't finalize anything yet. Not until this is resolved. It's a decision we made together." Tyrel's smile lit up as he thought of his girlfriend.

"I see." Torin fingered the envelope before he lifted his head again. He heard the doorbell and then the door opening. "The girls are here. They had planned to be."

Eilis appeared in the doorway, reaching to hug first Torin and then Tyrel. Tyrel had become an important part of the girls' lives and they treated him as an uncle.

"Torin? What are you up to?" Chani appeared next, with Brinn and Darbi following. "Our guys are with Tag and their friends, sorting out what they know."

———

"That's good." Torin smiled at them as he lifted up the envelope. "Frank dropped this off. We can make copies for each of us and then work through it."

Tyrel reached for the envelope, heading to make copies, Darbi beside him to sort them out. He frowned as he caught snatches of what the document contained. This was wilder than what he had even thought.

"Tyrel? Will this help?" Darbi's voice was low as she stared around, her eyes stopping on Torin.

"I pray that it does. We need to get your aunt back here and get Torin well again."

"What if Aunt Ash is really hurt and hasn't had treatment? What if she dies on us?" Darbi couldn't control her sobs.

Tyrel dropped the papers that he was holding and simply swept her into a hug, his eyes catching Torin. Torin nodded, knowing that Darbi was hurting. Ashlynn was the last link to their parents and they just needed their parents at this time.

Eilis turned from the room, moving towards the living room, standing in front of the window. She frowned as she saw the patrol car parked in front of the house and Frank walking their way. She drew in a deep breath. Something had happened and she was afraid. Her thoughts turned to a muddled prayer, certain that God would hear.

———

Chapter 35

Frank watched as the girls and Torin and Tyrel worked through the material. He simply stayed in the background, working on his cases as he could, stepping away to take phone calls or make them as he needed to. His supervisor had simply asked him to be there with them. He was fine that Frank was there for the time being. They had some ideas on where Ashlynn would be and were working through that.

Darbi moved through the room, studying the piles of paper on the floor. They had sorted through everything, read through it, and then compiled what they knew and what they suspected. They had come to the conclusion on a name and none of them liked it. Torin had reached out to Stephen, their conversation on speaker phone so that they could all hear.

"This doesn't make sense, Darbi." Eilis stood beside her cousin, an arm linked with hers. "What are we missing?"

"I don't know. I really don't know. I don't think it goes back as far as what that Stephen is saying. And it doesn't make a lot of sense that he would take the jewelry boxes and then return them."

Frank had been listening, knowing that Darbi had come right to the point on something that puzzled them all.

"Why would you say that, Darbi?" His question cut through the quiet in the room, bringing all eyes to the young lady.

Darbi shrugged, not sure why she had said that.

"I'm not sure, Frank. It just doesn't seem reasonable, does it? Why keep what he did? And the rings that were sent? Mom had them on that day. She would have had. She never took them off." Darbi looked up at a sound from Frank. "Frank?"

"I think that you just solved something, Darbi." Frank was away, his phone out, putting in a call to the medical examiner who he knew well. "George? You saw the ME reports from Ashlynn's brothers and their wives. We've talked. Can you remember if their jewelry was there? It was? That's what we thought. And you would not have removed it? No, I didn't think that you would. You would have kept it with their bodies if you had been the examiner. Was this documented, can you remember?"

George thought back through what he had read and then reached for his computer. He had a copy of it saved to hard drive. He pulled it up and scanned through it, pausing at one comment.

"Frank? Their jewelry was there. The ME mentions taking it off and putting it in envelopes to go to the funeral home for the family to decide what to do with it. But there is something else that I just noticed. It says that all the trauma didn't seem to come from the accident. That it was trauma that may have happened prior to that. But he could not be certain on that as they had no information of what had preceded their deaths."

Frank's steps froze as he heard that. This was what they had been looking for.

"Thanks, George. That's in all four reports?"

"It is, Frank. I hope that it helps. At the time I looked them over for you, I missed that. It is only one sentence in the midst of all the wording."

"That's okay, George. God wasn't ready for us to know that." Frank pocketed his phone, his thoughts troubled.

"Frank? You've discovered something." Torin stood beside him, realizing that something had just happened.

"I have. I had the ME here go back through the reports from their autopsies. They were dead before the accident. There was a sentence in each report about pre-accident trauma. And their jewelry was there with them, in envelopes to be taken to the funeral home."

"And your next step is to contact the funeral home to see if they received the jewelry. I don't think they did. Somehow, someone got to the body bags and removed it."

"I think that you are correct, Torin. I need to run back to the office and contact them. That patrol car stays. We have word that someone is trying to get to you today. We can't have that." Frank was away before Torin could say anything more.

Brinn had moved in, hearing the conversation. Her eyes closed for a moment as she thought through the implications of what had been said.

"Brinn?" Gareth's arms were around his wife, his eyes on her and then Torin. The other men moved past them, heading for the house. Brinn turned her head, noting that Evan, Tag, and Shea had appeared and their wives were with them. She smiled as she saw Garrett and Meg as well.

"I'm okay, Gareth. I just heard what Frank said, Torin. Is what he said right?"

"It is, Brinn. It is. We need to talk to the others, but first we need to eat and then spend time in prayer." Torin nodded at the car. "That car stays here, Frank said."

"It does? Then they must be close to finding Aunt Ash." She turned and walked away, leaving Gareth staring at Torin.

"Torin? What didn't you say?"

"I think Brinn understands without it being said. Someone removed the envelopes with the jewelry in them and kept them until now. That's a lot of planning and waiting." Torin's eyes slid shut and he swayed on his feet, Gareth's hand going out to steady him.

"We need to get you sitting down again, Torin." Gareth turned him for the house. "We'll talk. Dad has some information to add. And I hear from Evan that Emma is heading this way."

"She is? Good. She'll have information for us then. Before we go in, Gareth, thank you for being who you are. Ashlynn has talked about what you and Brinn went through. We are blessed to have each one of you men in our lives and in our family."

Tyrel watched his brother closely, knowing that he had heard some news which disturbed him greatly. He would talk with him later, he decided

Eilis stood against a wall, watching the commotion of so many people moving around. She drew in a deep shuddering breath. This is where Ashlynn shone, she knew, and no one knew where she was or if she would be back. That saddened her. Declan simply stood beside her, an arm around her, his prayer whispering in her ear.

Chapter 36

Ashlynn roused from the stupor that she had been in the last week. She scraped her hair back from her face, feeling grubby and unkempt. Her blurry eyes stared around, not sure what day it was or where she was. She had lost consciousness from the choking that she had been given that day, her screams cut off before they could be uttered. Ashlynn was sure that Torin was dead. She had visions of his body flying backwards to the ground, and then him not moving, with blood spreading on his chest.

Not feeling herself moved from her home, Ashlynn had been dropped onto the back seat of a car, a blanket draped over her. She had not felt the movement of the car as it moved away from her home. That would have frightened her if she had. She also did not feel herself dragged from the vehicle, gathered roughly up, and carried down a flight of stairs to a basement. Ashlynn was dropped onto a rough bunk and then the man backed away. The door was locked behind him, and he stood staring through the bars at her. This cell had been used before and he had no doubt that it would be used again. He knew nothing about what brought this woman here and he didn't want to know. His conscience was long dead.

The woman who had arranged for Ashlynn's abduction waited in the office, not turning as the man approached her, subservience in his demeanour.

"She's here?"

"She is. She's unconscious. She fought us."

———

"Of course, she did. What did you expect. And the man?"

"As far as we know, he's dead."

"Good, he deserves it." The woman didn't turn, merely waving him away. As his footsteps faded, she turned, an ugly, evil look on her face. All the years of planning and plotting had come to this point. Her thoughts turned even more evil. Ashlynn would pay for what she had been through and pay dearly. Her husband was dead and the woman was glad of that. That just left her nieces.

The woman paced before she gave an evil, vindictive laugh. Losing their aunt and not being able to find her body would be what they deserved. They had ruined her life, even though they didn't know about that, and they would pay for it. She cackled with evil glee at the thought.

She made the trek down the steps twice a day after that, to stand at the cell door and watch Ashlynn as she slept or laid unconscious. She wasn't sure which it was. She only knew that she had Ashlynn exactly where she wanted her and she would never let her go. Payback was coming to Ashlynn's family and he would pay dearly.

The man brought food and water down to Ashlynn three times a day, taking away the uneaten food and the empty water and juice bottles. He was growing concerned, something that was out of character for him. He heard the mutterings that his employer was giving, not caring that anyone was around, and knew the plans that were in place for

Ashlynn. Beginning to think through what was going on, the man was having second thoughts about what was happening. As far as he knew, Ashlynn had done nothing to warrant her treatment. He walked away that day, lost in thought. He felt that he had to do something but wasn't sure what that something was. He would need to act soon, he knew, given the plans that were in place for Ashlynn.

Ashlynn sat up on the side of the bunk, her head spinning from that movement. She wasn't sure where she was or even who she was. Her eyes searched the room, seeing the bars on the door and then the barred window. A jail cell, she thought, and why? She hadn't done anything that would warrant being locked up. Only, she decided at last, it wasn't a regular jail. Ashlynn stumbled to her feet, making her way to the window. Her hands curled around the bars as she held herself upright. Staring through the window, Ashlynn blinked. She thought that she knew the area, the place, but it couldn't be. The owners would not do this. At least, she didn't think that they would.

She didn't turn as she heard the lock click and heard movement behind her. The sound of a tray sliding onto a table startled her for a moment and then the door lock clicked behind her. The footsteps faded into the distance as the man walked away and up the stairs.

Turning at last, Ashlynn searched for the man, not seeing him. She made her way slowly to the tray, seeing the sandwich, fruit, and water there. She reached for the water, uncapping it and drinking deeply. She sighed to herself before she headed for the rough ensuite, the water tap on the sink turned on to run as hot as she thought that she could stand. Her face was washed and she felt slightly more awake.

Snuggling down under the torn blanket, Ashlynn turned her thoughts to Torin. She began to grieve, sure that he was dead. There was no way that he could have survived that bullet, she thought. She wept, her weeping finally ending as she slept.

The man returned for the tray, standing for a moment before he reached for it. He knew that the woman was away for a few days. This would be the opportunity for Ashlynn to escape. He would help in that and then disappear.

Ashlynn roused in the early morning light, slightly more awake than she had been. She stared at the tray sitting there, concerned that the man had been around when she was asleep. Staring at the window, she saw that it was early morning. Rising, she walked to the tray, seeing that there were three sandwiches and that many water bottles, as well as a knapsack sitting on the table. She frowned. This was not what she had expected.

Thoughtfully, she turned to the door. Ashlynn's hand reached for the door, finding it opening under her touch. Surprised, she waited, her head tilted as she listened. There was no movement upstairs. She crept from the room, having retrieved the rough blanket and stuffing it and the food and water in the knapsack. Staring down at her feet, Ashlynn was glad that she still had her shoes on.

Moving as silently as she could, Ashlynn placed one foot at a time on the stairs, wincing as she heard the slight squeak of one and waiting for someone to appear. When no one appeared, she crept up each step, her hand reaching for the door to shove it open. She then peeked around the mudroom and frowned. This was a high-end house, Ashlynn decided. She reached for the knob to the outside door, her movements quiet and careful. The door opened and she stepped through into the early morning light.

Realizing that it was only around four in the morning, Ashlynn paused for a moment, a prayer rising from her.

Lord, You freed me. Now, I just need to find my way home. Or to safety of some kind. I have no idea where I am or how long it has been. I need to find someone. Only I have no idea who. And I just know that my beloved Torin is dead. He couldn't have survived that shot. Not where he was hit. Please, Lord, I need to go on with my life. Keep my girls safe, that's all I ask. Let us end this as soon as we can. I can't let them go through anything more.

Chapter 37

Stepping quietly across the lawn, Ashlynn made her way towards the road that she could see. She realized that she was out in the country. Only she had no idea where exactly that was. There was nothing that showed her that. She stumbled as she walked, her feet moving one in front of the other in automatic steps. She sank to the ground as one point, finding shelter under a tree. A car moved past her, and Ashlynn shrank back into the ground. She didn't want to be seen not sure who was a friend or who was an enemy.

Night found her searching for a place to sleep. Her eyes could barely stay open. Her feet hurt and she would barely put one in front of the other. She found a shack and hesitated before she pushed open the door. It was empty but musty smelling. That didn't matter to Ashlynn. It was safety and shelter and that was all that mattered. She knew that God had provided it for her. Wrapping the blanket around her, Ashlynn settled herself into a corner, the knapsack tucked tight to her. She slept, not seeing the critters that shared her shelter stopping to study her and then deciding that she mean them no harm.

The next day was a repeat of the first day. Ashlynn had no idea where she was or even if she was headed in the right direction. The second night was spent as the first one had been. Only this time she found shelter in a barn, snuggling down in loose straw, the blanket pulled over her. She slept, exhausted beyond what she ever had been, but confident that God was there, leading her home.

Early the next morning, the door to the barn swung open, and two men appeared in the doorway. They shared a look before they began searching.

"Matt? Here. Ashlynn's here. She's sleeping." Micah knelt beside her, a hand out to brush her hair from her face. "How long has she been walking?"

"A couple of days from what we were told." Matt, the paramedic on Abe's team, reached to gently shake Ashlynn awake.

Ashlynn shot up, fear making her scream. She stared at the men even as she fought to free herself from the blanket and then scramble backwards until she hit a pile of straw bales. Her eyes darted between Matt and Micah, not recognizing them.

Matt's hand went up even as Micah settled back on his feels. Her scream had startled them, causing them to jump backwards a bit.

"Ashlynn? It's okay. You're safe. You are safe." Matt waited patiently for Ashlynn to calm down, her silence not worrying him. He knew that she was afraid and that they had startled her. He prayed for her as well. That was a given with Abe's team. They prayed for everyone that they went in to retrieve and bring back to safety.

Ashlynn blinked rapidly, her heart rate returning to normal. Her eyes shifted between the men before recognition.

"Micah? Matt? What are you doing here? Am I really safe?" Ashlynn sank back to the straw and reached for her knapsack, clutching it close to her, afraid to let it go unless she had no other water or food to get her home.

"We were looking for you. And we found you." Matt grinned at her. "Now, do you want to go home?"

"You were? How did you find me?" Ashlynn was on her feet, heading for the door, not waiting for the men to stand.

"Ashlynn! Wait!" Micah was at her side, his hand on her arm. "We need to be careful. We don't know if someone has been following you or not. We've been tracking you since yesterday afternoon."

"You have been? How did you know where I was?" She waited impatiently for Micah to walk through the door and then look back through to motion them forward. Matt's hand on her arm steadied her on her feet.

"We received word that you were in the area. We split up into teams to search for you. We were the ones to find you." Matt followed Ashlynn as they walked off. "We have a vehicle near here. That will get you back to your family."

Ashlynn stopped suddenly, so suddenly that Matt ran into her by accident. His hands went up to steady her.

"Ashlynn?" He tilted his head to watch her face. "Ashlynn?"

"Torin? He's dead, isn't he?" She couldn't control her tears and sobs.

"Torin?" Micah shared a look with Matt. "No, Ashlynn. He's alive. Sure, he was shot but God kept him alive. We'll get you to him. First, we need to get you to the hospital for assessment, to the police to give your statement, and then we'll get you to your home. Your nieces and their husbands have been there over the last couple of days, working to solve your mystery. And they have made strides in doing that."

Ashlynn simply nodded, her thoughts muddled. To hear that Torin was still alive would take an adjustment of her thoughts. She praised God that he was but was saddened that he had been hurt. She settled back on the seat in the car, her tears still flowing. Matt handed her a bottle of juice, watching her carefully to assess her health. Micah shared a look with him before he drove off.

Abe stood in the emergency department of the hospital, Micah beside him. He was thankful that Ashlynn had been found and was relatively unhurt. Frank was with her, taking her statement.

"How far from the house did you find her?" Abe's voice was quiet.

"About ten miles or so. We were looking for buildings and searching them. God led us to that one." Micah was tired but wouldn't seek any rest until Ashlynn was back with her family. "She was convinced that Torin was dead. She's needing to work through that."

——

"She will. We'll get Darci to speak with her. Now, when she's free, we'll get her home. Torin was to be at the office for a while this morning, he said, but would be home around noon. Her nieces are at work but are planning to work with him tonight again on the mystery. They've been making headway in that."

"They have? That doesn't surprise me. Kat has been speaking with Eilis, giving her as much family history as she can. What she can't give them she's passing on to Frank and Adam." Micah sighed. "This goes back to far, too far for Ashlynn to have even been aware of it."

"It does, but it ends now. Frank told me that he had word the woman is heading back to town in the next couple of days. He's working to finalize all his information and obtain his search warrants." Abe's eyes went to the curtain on the cubicle, seeing it open and Ashlynn appear, Frank at her side. Frank's head shook slightly. Abe sighed. This was where it got dangerous, when it was almost over.

Chapter 38

His heart heavy, Torin stood on the back porch, staring into the distance, feeling the cooling breeze from the west. He was missing his bride, just wishing that he knew where Ashlynn was. He was afraid that she was dead and would never come back to him, that they would never find her body. His heart cried out to God constantly, not finding the peace that he needed. That afternoon, he finally was just quiet, waiting on God, feeling the peace that he had been seeking flowing into his heart.

He heard the door open and close behind him and then soft footsteps that stopped behind him. He thought it was one of his family or one of the girls or a friend. He didn't turn. When the person didn't speak, he spoke.

"Who is it?" When the person didn't speak, he turned, freezing as he faced the person in front of him. "Ashlynn!" His sob broke the stillness as Ashlynn sprang towards him, to be caught close to his heart.

Their tears shook both their bodies, neither willing to let the other go. Torin finally leaned back to stare down at her beloved face. He reached to kiss her before he leaned back once more.

"Ashlynn? Where did you come from?" Torin turned her back towards the house, not realizing that Abe and his men were roaming outside, just keeping an eye out for them.

"Matt and Micah found me. I was walking home, I guess. I spent two nights hiding from anyone. It's okay, we can talk about it. Frank has my statement. Only it's not much of one. I have no idea who took me or why. I woke up in a cell in a basement. Two days ago, the door was left unlocked and I just walked away." Ashlynn sighed, exhaustion hitting her hard. "I need to clean up, love."

"I know you do. Here, let's get you cleaned up. Then you can decide where you want to be and if you want anything to eat." Torin was reluctant to let her out of his sight but he did need to speak with Abe.

Abe turned as Torin approached him, reaching for the carafe and poured them both a mug of coffee before he pointed to the living room.

"In there, Torin. You'll be able to hear Ashlynn from there." Abe sat, unsure how much that he could tell him.

"What can you tell me?" Torin was restless, wanting to hear what he could be told but not certain that he should.

"Micah and Matt tracked her down in a barn early this morning. They brought her to the hospital and then had Frank come in to get her statement. She was not that far from here, about twenty miles. Matt thinks that she had walked about ten miles in the two days that she was free."

"Ten miles? That far?" Torin's eyes slid closed. "She was that far from here?"

"She was. We suspect that she would have walked back here, as hard as it would have been on her. She would not have taken a ride, not sure who that she could trust." Abe was tired as well, having spent the night before searching.

"Thank you, Abe, and to your team as well. You have proven to be true friends for us." Torin's hand went up. "I know that this is what you do, but you still have our thanks." Torin was on his feet, wrapping Ashlynn to him and then sitting down, his bride tucked close to him.

"Ashlynn? You're okay?" Abe smiled as she stared at him and then shook her head. "No, I didn't think that you would be. Darci is willing to speak with you when you're ready. She has a burden for you and for her to have that, she needs to act."

"Thank her for me. For now, I just need to be here with Torin." She sighed. "And the girls. They'll be here with us, won't they?"

"They will be. They've been around every night, working through the information that we have. Stephen was around that Saturday and left information for us. Frank has proven it all, I think, from what he said. He's working on search warrants and arrest warrants."

"From what he told me, those should be in place in the next forty-eight hours. Your captor, Ashlynn, was a woman. She's been out of town for the last three days and not expected back until tomorrow. By that time, Frank will be ready to move in."

"That's sounds good." Ashlynn yawned and then turned her face against Torin's chest, falling asleep in an instance.

Torin's gaze was on her, missing Abe's smile. Abe was on his feet, heading for the door, finding Murphy waiting for him. A quiet conversation ensued between the two men and then Murphy headed for the others.

Abe returned to stand for a moment, his eyes on Torin, before he spoke.

"Torin? We're heading home. Frank has a patrol car here for now."

Torin nodded, not sure if Abe would be back or not, but glad to have had him there.

Three hours later, Torin heard a tap at the door and then footsteps heading towards him. He gave a brief smile. All four of the ladies were there, he thought. He tilted his head to look back at them, seeing the instance that they saw their aunt.

"Torin?" Brinn was on her knees beside the couch, her hand out but not quite touching her aunt. "When did Aunt Ash get home?"

"Around noon. Abe's men found her. It's okay. She's safe." Torin smiled through tears as he saw the four young ladies weeping. "She's tired but she's not harmed."

"Not physically." Chani was adamant on that. She sank into a chair, her eyes on her aunt, thankful that she was home but worried about what had happened to her.

Ashlynn stirred an hour later, her senses telling her that she was not alone. She cracked open her eyes, finding herself still in Torin's arms. She pushed against him to sit upright, pushing at her hair, finding all eyes on her. She sighed to herself. Ashlynn knew that she had to speak with them, but was reluctant to tell them.

"Aunt Ash?" Eilis spoke from where she had seated herself on the floor near Torin's feet. She held out a bottle of juice which Ashlynn took. "Are you okay?"

"Thank you. I am. Let me just get my bearings and I'll tell you what happened. Is Frank around?" She searched the room, not seeing him.

"He's not, sweetheart. He's working on the warrants that they need. Right now, it is only the woman who held you captive that they are trying to find. She's been out of the country and is flying back in tomorrow. They'll arrest her at the airport. Anyone who was working with her has been arrested. And you are safe. That is guaranteed. They won't let her near you."

"Thank you, love." Ashlynn settled back against him, her eyes finding each one of her nieces and their guys. "I don't know why she did this. I was unconscious for much of the time that I was away. They had choked me to unconsciousness when they took me. I thought until this morning that Torin was dead." She heard the indrawn breaths and soft comments as she said that. "Anyway, Frank is working through the details. He thanks you for what you have given him and said that it helped. Now, we need to eat. I can't remember eating in a week." She was on her feet, heading for the kitchen, leaving them staring after her.

Brinn began to laugh, bringing eyes to her face, as she rose as well, the other three ladies with her.

"Aunt Ash has spoken. We eat. Then we pray. Then we talk."

Frank stood in the entryway, hearing the conversation and the laughter, a smile crossing his face. It was now early evening. The woman had returned early and been arrested as she stepped through customs at the airport, despite her protests. Her questioning would come in the next few days but Frank was confident that they had everyone. Adam had agreed. There was no one else that this family had to fear.

Turning as he heard footsteps, Frank stared at his friend. Ashlynn had approached quietly, not saying anything. He simply reached to hug his longtime friend.

"You're okay, Ash?"

She nodded as she stepped backwards.

"I am, thank you. Sue has called. We're going to get together in a couple of days, just to spend some time together without any worries. I need that."

"You do. Now, I have word. We arrested her tonight, Ashlynn." Frank waited as she absorbed his words.

Ashlynn nodded, her thoughts troubled for a moment.

"Thank you for that, Frank. I want to know why, but that will take a couple of days I know. It is a relief to know that it is over. You'll need to finish off the investigation. How be we all meet on Saturday to hear what you can tell us?"

"That works. Now, how be we find your family? I could use some downtime, just for the night. You're safe, your girls are safe, and that is all that matters tonight."

Frank walked towards the kitchen, leaving Ashlynn staring after him. She turned and walked to the sunroom, finding the rocker that she had claimed. Her tears started, tears of healing and regret. She missed her parents, her brothers, and their wives, and just needed time to come to terms with what she knew was coming. Frank had dropped some hints when they spoke earlier that day.

Torin found her at last, simply scooping her into his arms and then sitting in the rocker, his toe setting it in motion. Words were not needed, not that night. They would talk but for now they were content just to sit with one another, safe at home with each other.

Chapter 39

That Saturday, Frank looked around Torin's backyard, seeing who all had appeared. Torin and Ashlynn stood near the fountain in the centre of the yard, his parents nearby. Tyrel and Lily were at the back of the years, with Flynn's family. He knew that Gareth's family, Ronan's family, and Declan's family were there as well. The four girls as Ashlynn called them and their husbands were preparing a meal, insisting that was what they wanted to do.

At last, Frank set his mug down and then stood, reaching for the folder he had set to one side. He had the answers that they needed and wanted. He had not been prepared for what he had found. Adam had not been either. They had investigated closely and researched their work many times. They had sat back, looked at one another and shook their heads.

He searched the faces that had turned to him. He found Gareth's eyes and nodded. Gareth was on his feet, his eyes closed as he prayed. This was needed, he knew. Sitting once more, he reached for Meg's hand. His eyes remained closed as others in the group picked up the chain of prayer. He could feel God's presence there. His eyes opened for a moment as he watched Torin and Ashlynn, finding Torin's arm holding his bride close to him.

Frank turned to Torin and Ashlynn, at a loss for words for a moment. Ashlynn watched him before her eyes moved to Sue, who nodded. Sue and Ashlynn had spoken the day before and prayed together. Sue knew that Ashlynn was ready to hear the answers of what had troubled the family for fifteen years or more, what had taken away Ashlynn's early life as a college graduate and made her into a mother. She was happy now, Sue knew, with the one who God had prepared for her.

"Frank? What do you have to say?" Ashlynn's voice was controlled and taut, showing the tight control that she had her emotions under.

"I'm not sure where to start, Ashlynn, girls. It goes back to before your brothers died. The woman who abducted you and held you captive? She is involved in that. Her name is Wilhelmina Winston. She knew your father and mother but it wasn't because of them that you brothers were killed. Aaron and Adam were killed because of spite. That seems so trite to say that. I'll come to the reasons for it.

"As we suspected, your brothers and their wives were deceased before the car accident. That was missed in the initial investigation even though it was in the medical examiner's report. The investigator from your home town didn't have the correct reports. The ones that he was given had been tampered with. I spoke with him late last week and he was shocked. He is not sure what other evidence has been tampered with at this time. We think that some of it has been.

"Now, for what you each received that was your parents? Winston has stated that she was responsible for that. She was able to get into your homes and retrieve what she wanted from there. She is the one who had the garages packed up and then taken to the landfill site. I'm sorry that we can't retrieve anything from there. She also was able to tamper with the body bags that held your family and take the envelopes with the jewelry. She banked on you being too emotional and upset to notice that the jewelry was missing.

"Stephen Steele was able to provide some insight into what happened. Your father, Ashlynn, and your grandfather, girls, was a successful businessman. He was a printer, well thought of in the community. He would stand for nothing that was dishonest coming through his business. Winston tried to get him to print some false information and brochures for him years before he died. He refused and threatened her with charges if it ever came out what she was saying. She held that against him for years. When he passed away, she turned her attention to your brothers, Ashlynn. You were too young for her to go after. Your brother, Adam, took over the business from your father. Aaron was in the bank.

"This is where her mind twisted. She decided that she would get back at Aaron and Adam by having counterfeit money printed at the business and then coming through the bank. Only she was never able to get into the business. Not one of the employees would help her. That made her resentment grow and her mind twisted. She decided that your brothers needed to pay. She had them beaten that night, your mothers beaten as well. What she didn't realize was that the men went too far. I'm sorry that your parents died from that. Those men have long since disappeared. We have searched for them. We do know their names and have sent out bulletins across Canada. If they are still alive, we will find them.

"Her plans were to kill you, to leave your family to grieve for the rest of their lives. Your body was not to be ever found from what the documentation we have found has stated. God watched over you that day, Ashlynn. And we have no idea who left the door unlocked that morning.

"Torin, you were taken just for spite. Winston seemed to connect you two for whatever reason. And apparently she had approached your foundation for aid years ago and was refused. That has festered in her mind for all this time.

"Now, as to Winston, she is not talking. We have ample proof of what she has done over the years. That includes the counterfeiting and other crimes which will come out when the charges are laid. She is not talking as yet, but we're working on the charges.

"I'm sorry, once more, Ashlynn, that it has taken this long to solve this. I wish that we could have solved it before it came to this."

Ashlynn rose to hug him before she turned to her nieces.

"It's okay, Frank. God is in control. This has been in His timing."

"Thank you, Ashlynn." Frank moved away but still watched her closely before his attention went to the girls. They were in shock, as he would suspect them to be.

It was a quiet group that finally broke up. Each of the girls hugged their aunt tightly, almost not wanting to let go.

Torin found her later, standing on the back porch, her hands resting on the railing. He simply wrapped her into his arms and held her. Night had fallen and they could hear the night sounds around them.

"Okay, sweetheart?" Torin thought that she was but he had to check with her.

"I am, Torin. I think that I finally am. There has always been that question as to why Aaron and Adam died. It hurts to hear why but God is here with us. He'll walk us through the next few months." She leaned back against him.

"That He will." Torin stepped back, his eyes on her. "I'll be in the house when you're ready to come in."

Torin stepped back into the house, leaning against a wall in the kitchen, just waiting. He kept his love and her girls in his prayers, knowing that God was hearing and would heal. Ashlynn finally returned to the house, shutting and locking the door behind her. She saw him waiting and simply walked into his hug. She was home and safe and with the man who she loved and adored and was loved and adored in return.

Two years had passed since the adventure had ended for Ashlynn and Torin. Life had gone on. Ashlynn was still working but was planning on leaving soon. Gerry would miss her but was happy for her in her next adventure.

Ashlynn stood on their back porch, a contented smile on her face. Her nieces were in the yard as were their guys and the families who had become part of her life. She watched as Brinn cuddled her six-month-old son, Aaron. Chani was to become a mother in a month or so, a daughter that they planned to call Cait. Darbi's three-month-old daughter, Heidi, was in her grandmother's arms. Her attention turned to Eilis. Eilis had told her that morning that they were expecting in about six months and that if it was a boy, they would name him Adam. Ashlynn had hugged her niece, happy for her.

Torin's arms came around his bride as he still referred to her as. He was happy, more content than he ever thought he could be. His hands rested on Ashlynn's abdomen, feeling their child moving. She had laughed at him that morning when he asked her if the baby would arrive that day. She had shrugged and simply told him that it was God's timing.

Ashlynn turned in Torin's arms, hugging him. Neither one of them had thought about being parents, thinking that they were too old but it seemed as if God had other ideas. They were prayed for, they knew, and prayed for their friends and family in return.

"Okay, sweetheart?"

"I am, love, and I know that you are. We went through so much but it brought us closer together. God has been gracious to us. You have been the lamp in my life and in so many others. You are ready to respond to anyone without being asked. Thank you for that."

Ashlynn hugged him tighter.

"You are my rock, love, the one who keeps me grounded. I thought that my life was over. I was ready to spend the rest of my life on my own. God had other plans."

"He did at that, sweetheart. I am glad that we met and are now together. I would be lost without you."

Ashlynn reached for his kiss, knowing that he wanted to say more but just couldn't put it into words.

"Let's go spend time with our families, Torin. We are blessed with so many in our lives. I am glad that I came to this town. I never really fit into that other town. And I am also glad that we had nothing to do with its founding. That would have been so hard to deal with."

"It would have been, but you would have been fine. That's how God works."

The girls swarmed towards their aunt, hugging her, laughing at her comments. They had been a group of girls that had expanded as they married. They would not have traded their life with their aunt, unless it had meant that their parents were still alive. They all stated that they hadn't wanted to be raised by anyone other than their Aunt Ash.

A week later, Torin approached Ashlynn as she sat in the sunroom, a bundle in her arms. He sat beside her, reaching to kiss her, before a finger came out to lightly move the blanket. Their son had been born six days ago, a son who they called Andrew Troye after his grandfathers. Torin then reached for his daughter, asleep in the basinet beside the love seat. His smile grew as he watched her yawn before Ashlynn laughed softly. Little Abigayle Heather was the image of her mother, Torin maintained.

The couple had not expected to have twins but they were content. They had not told anyone that they would be blessed with two, but they knew that the littles ones were loved and wanted in the families. They also knew that God had blessed them mightily with their littles ones, their families, and their friends.

Ashlynn had decided to resign from work, simply stating to Gerry that her life had now changed direction. He had agreed, only asking if she would be willing to work on a contract basis. She had looked at him and then told him she would discuss it with Torin and let him know. He had simply nodded.

Looking around her home, Ashlynn was content in a way that she had never been. She had never dreamed that she would marry and be a mother. Those were dreams that she had tucked away in the deep recesses of her heart, not expecting that God would honour her dream. Torin had told her that he had felt the same. Their lives were complete now and they

were ready to move forward, raising their children and
serving God where He placed them.

Thank you for reaching for Ashlynn and Torin's story, the last in the series of His Ladies with the Lamps. It has been a series that was a number of years in the making but one that I always wanted to write. I am the aunt of four nieces (and one nephew). So it just sort of fit into my life.

Ashlynn and Torin went through a lot, but their love for one another and their love and faith in God shone through. I had not planned their story. My unruly characters never let me do that. Instead, they just let me come along for the ride, as wild as it can be at times. And it always turns out to be the best story for the characters.

The parable of the wise virgins has always been a favourite of mine. I can remember as a child hearing our pastor at the time preach a sermon on it. That has stuck with me. My father would often mention it. Dad was a carpenter but build furniture for me in his later years. He built me a stand for my keyboard, an organ stand that he called it. It has a high back with a music book rack, a roll top cover, storage on either end. I treasure it because it was something that he designed and created, a one of a kind piece. When he did it, he included some very precious things on it. On the back underneath the keyboard portion are seven pieces of wood. These he said were the seven churches in Revelations. On the top of the book rack, he carefully handcrafted what look like lamp chimneys. There are five. These he told me were the five wise virgins from the parable. Dad spent a lot of time in thought but never talked a lot about what he was discovering in Scripture. When he did, it was something like this. Dad graduated to heaven in 2012, about two and a half years after Mom. They are missed so very much.

As to the characters that have walked into the story, Abe and Emma and their team's stories are in *His Guardians*. Doug and Darci's story is *The Heart of a Lion*. The other friends that showed up are in *His Dreamseekers* and *His Searchers*.

When you go through difficulties, remember that you are not alone. God is there every step of the way. When you cannot put your prayers into words, the Spirit prays for you. That is a promise that never fails.

God bless each one of you. May God enrich your lives as you serve Him. Be the lamp in the darkness of this world, ready to respond when He calls you to.

Ronna